A Handful of Worldliness
An Edwina Goodman Mystery
by
Elissa Grodin

For information, email Cozy Cat Press, cozycatpress@aol.com or visit our website at: www.cozycatpress.com

COZY CAT
PRESS

ISBN: 978-1-946063-76-2
Printed in the United States of America

10 9 8 7 6 5 4 3 2 1

Thank you to my technical advisors on this book.

Howard Eison, MD, FCCP, FACP, provided invaluable medical guidance and cone snail research.

Joe Kenda (the "Homicide Hunter"), retired police lieutenant, generously—and often with humor—answered my questions about police matters and procedures.

Tory Johnson and Amy Kahn Russell offered enormously useful information about what it's like to be in front of the home shopping cameras.

Dan Wing advised me about how to build a mountain trail.

And, Assistant Professor of Physics at The University of Connecticut, Cara Battersby, Ph.D., gave me a peek into the heart and mind of Edwina.

Every leaf speaks bliss to me, fluttering from the autumn tree.
~ Emily Bronte

$$a = (vf - vi) / (tf - ti)$$
~ Isaac Newton, on the acceleration of a falling leaf

Chapter 1

A man without ethics is a wild beast loosed upon this
world.
~ Albert Camus

He had imagined the scene countless times. He
would hasten down a flight of steps to the lower level
of the building, his expensive brogues clicking a merry
rhythm along the way. He would find his way through a
maze of dimly lit corridors, lined with peeling, faded,
linoleum tiles. The light fixtures would be dusty.
Indeed, the general décor of the subterranean hidey-
hole was bound to receive little attention, and suggest
nothing of the Georgian grandeur of the rest of the
building, where one floor above, the stately entrance
ushered visitors in through Greek columns flanking a
classical, limestone lintel. Inside, tall stained glass
windows encircled a vaulted vestibule that led into a
soaring, marble entry hall.

He would perhaps arrive at a nondescript, metal door
at the end of a corridor, where he would find a
discreetly placed keypad. He would punch in a code.
His cell phone would need to be placed in a lead lined
cabinet for security purposes. A dreary outer office
would be appointed with dated wallpaper and drab, out-
of-date furnishings.

But, he mustn't get ahead of himself with his little
daydreams! He wasn't officially part of the
organization, yet. Still, there seemed little room for
doubt that The Agency would bring him on board once

they had the opportunity to review his ideas regarding national security in this era of terrorism. He hardly allowed the possibility that the Agency might reject him to cross his mind; it was all but unimaginable.

He envisioned computer terminals and keyboards crowding the Secure Communications Room – from where he would make contact with the Agency – filled with scads of cables and wires trailing messily everywhere, and a spare amount of barely comfortable, utilitarian furniture.

He had conjured up this victory scene countless times. Some nights, he even dreamed about it. He wondered how close the landscape in his imagination would come to the real place.

Chapter 2

He who hoards much loses much.
~ Laozi

Known around town as Cousin Honey for her long, amber colored hair, Amaleen Stuckey had lived in Crawford, Tennessee, all her fifty-three years, and on the whole, life there had been good to her. She enjoyed her job at the post office, and the ease of living right across the street in her cozy apartment above Dalyrimple's Hardware Store. Amaleen had never married, nor wanted to, had never been asked, and had no children. Still, the word 'spinster' made her feel uneasy, and she cringed whenever she heard it spoken, but happily for Amaleen, the term seemed gradually to be going out of style.

Besides her work at the post office, Amaleen's life revolved around her slavish devotion to GHN (*Gotta Have It Now!*), the 24/7 television shopping channel, whose coterie of female hosts were wizards in the mastery of generating the ceaseless, uplifting, chatter that made Amaleen feel loved, no matter what else was going on in her life. She marveled at these women's abilities to cast a spell of well-being and order over everything. For that reason, she kept a small TV secreted under the counter at the post office, and it was always tuned to GHN. At any given time she was able to let her customers know what was being presented on the air.

"Morning, Miss Pickering," Amaleen said. "Remember when we were discussing juicers last week? They're showing a real nice combination juice extractor-five-speed-blender on GHN right now at a reduced price. You might want to get home and check that out."

At home, Amaleen kept the television in her bedroom tuned to GHN even during the night when she slept. It was like a steady dose of Prozac that softened the terrifying feelings of aloneness and emptiness she kept stowed away. The more banal the banter, the more it comforted her, and the more it eased her hypertension. An uncomplicated, relaxing, on-air conversation about the virtues of a snap closure versus a button closure on a French, terry cloth jacket lowered Amaleen's stress level every time. Or when the ladies demonstrated Velcro closures on footwear. The sound of that gentle crunching was like catnip to her.

GHN offered her a place to belong, to stay as long as she liked, and it asked very little of her in return. Over time she had come to think of the GHN presenters as something akin to personal friends. The carefree presenters were always having so much fun—laughing and joking around, as if they were at a party. They were so thoughtful and friendly, full of good advice about all sorts of things. Just exactly what you wanted in a virtual friend.

"Worrying is like being on a rocking horse," one of Amaleen's favorite hosts said during a presentation of lavender-scented bathroom deodorizer, "it keeps you going, but it doesn't get you anywhere."

Amaleen relished these bits of wisdom, and the feeling of being part of something bigger than herself—part of this sisterhood who appreciated beautiful things—the finer things in life. And, as if that weren't enough of a blessing in Amaleen's life, her love of GHN fit neatly into her other hobby: hoarding.

The landscape of her cramped apartment, stuffed as it was with unopened GHN packages in every room, many of them stacked all the way to the ceiling, was alarming to everyone except Amaleen. This hadn't been much of a problem in recent years, since she no longer cared to invite anybody over. There were small inconveniences to her, of course, like the fact that the boxes and packages had gradually cut off the view of Main Street through the picture window in her living room, the apartment's main source of natural light. Her solution was to purchase a few extra lamps from GHN, which she placed atop boxes, and kept turned on even on the sunniest days. Her favorite new lighting fixture was in the shape of a quaint, old-fashioned post office with a striped awning. She had picked it up on sale for three easy payments of only $29.98.

Her approach to keeping years of unopened purchases organized was alphabetical, by the first letter of the item, with boxes marked clearly in her large, childish scrawl. Amaleen was nothing if not systematic in her approach to sorting things. Years of working at the post office had honed these skills. So, for example, Thaddeus The Teddy Bear was grouped with a taffeta tablecloth; a Tiffany style lamp; a toaster oven; a tea maker; tea towels; a tanning kit; and so on. In the 'M's you would find a multifunction grill pan; melamine measuring cup set; microfiber mops; meat tenderizing mallet; men's grooming kit; Marcy's mud mask mix; a mini-mascara set from Marguerite Beauty. Amaleen's favorite section was the S's, which she sometimes read aloud for fun, so she could enjoy hearing the calming, sibilant sounds: Set of six saucepans; Sugar Plum Fairy Holiday Candlesticks; Sequin embellished Sweatshirt; Spa-Scented Candle Set; Snowy Night Snow Globe;

Six-quart steamer; Sea Glass Wind Chimes; Santa's Secret Nightlight; Sapphire-Sparkle Slippers; Shamrock Sheet Set; Sherri's Superior Silicone Sponges; and so on. And, on those occasions when she needed a gift for someone, she browsed leisurely through the stacks for the perfect present, just as she would in a real store. There was something for everyone there, and she didn't even have to leave the house to find it.

Perhaps a few people in her orbit knew a red flag when they saw one, but no one chose to say anything about it. For the most part, Amaleen's friends and family considered her little hobby a harmless pastime, but they were mindful not to use the word 'hoarder' in her presence.

Cousin Honey's just a happy packrat, they would say. *Bless her heart!*

Amaleen experienced no particular problems related to her hoarding habit, even though the apartment was largely impassable except for the narrow footpath that wound through the rooms, and created a sort of canyon effect. Her cramped quarters would have appeared to others as chaotic, but her home did not feel the least bit shambolic to Amaleen. On the contrary; everything had its proper place, and everything was under control. And, on nights when she had trouble sleeping, Amaleen wandered through this little canyon, her own, magical, yellow-brick road. It gave her a feeling of well-being and peace of mind to breathe in the scent of packing materials, and to know there would always be new arrivals to look forward to. Every time another package arrived it felt like Christmas.

Nor did it pose a problem for her that she had not been able to use her stove in years, blocked off from access as it had become by piles of boxes. Amaleen had never particularly enjoyed cooking, anyway. Once the stove became unreachable, she purchased GHN's

junior-sized microwave oven—the 'dormitory special'–
–for two payments of $22.49. It sat on a folding card
table with one chair tucked under it, perfectly adequate
for the microwave meals she enjoyed. She successfully
maintained use of the refrigerator, taking care that there
was enough space to open the door a third of the way,
just the right amount of room to be able to reach inside
for whatever she needed. Attached with magnets to the
front of the fridge she kept the GHN schedule, and two
8 x 10 photos of her favorite presenters, Fanny
Spendlove and Mary Lou Flowers. She was in the habit
of sending them little gifts and cards from time to time,
with the happy knowledge that the jokes and poems she
posted on their websites brightened their long days at
the network.

Lately, Amaleen had been giving thought to the
eventuality that one day she would run out of room in
her apartment for new packages. The answer to her
prayers came when an old high school classmate, Joby
Fulcher, opened up a mini-storage facility right outside
of town. Amaleen signed up as Joby's first customer.
She proudly held the keys to two brand new, storage
units, with plenty of space for years of GHN packages
to come, in a clean, secure, temperature controlled
environment. The relief and peace of mind Joby's new
storage facility gave her was immeasurable, and she
told him so every time he came into the post office.

Tucked up in bed for the night with a mug of hot
chocolate piled high with mini-marshmallows, Amaleen
watched her idol.

"This is an amazing, amazing, iconic purse," Fanny
Spendlove said in her honeyed voice, pushing back her
waved tresses with long, painted fingernails. "You have
literally got to own this bag! I hate to think how you'll
feel if you miss out on this opportunity, before it sells

out at this amazing, one-time price! It's a must-have, ladies!"

Gosh! How glamorous Fanny looks in that beaded evening gown, Amaleen thought.

"Now, before I take you on a tour of all the incredible, incredible details this amazing bag has to offer," Fanny said, "I want to remind you all that my dear friend, Mary Lou Flowers, will be with you next hour with some new fashion essentials from GHN's very own, in-house designer, Sue Shamrack, so please be sure to stay tuned for that! Sue's clothing line has been exclusive to GHN for twenty-two years. Don't bother trying to find any of her fabulous fashion items or jewelry in those brick-and-mortar mausoleums at the mall! When you can order beautiful clothes like these— without the hassle of having to try things on in those yucky fitting rooms—not to mention the incredible convenience of having your new items delivered right to your door, what's not to love about Sue Shamrack and GHN!"

"Now, say it with me, ladies!" Fanny smiled. "You all know my mantra by now! Here we go, out loud and proud!"

Amaleen sat up in bed, and chanted along with Fanny, "STORES WITH DOORS! OH! WHAT BORES!"

"How 'bout it, Miss Mary Lou?" Fanny beamed.

A second camera picked up Mary Lou Flowers on the adjacent set, where she stood next to a rack of brightly colored clothing items, laughing and clapping her hands in appreciation of Fanny's rally cry. Mary Lou wore a bright, yellow dress that rode up on her hips despite repeated efforts to tug it into place. The dress clashed with the miscalculated shade of Mary Lou's makeup (too dark and too much orange). This color combination gave her a jarringly theatrical look.

"You got that right!" Mary Lou laughed, waving at camera 2. "Sue Shamrack has come up with some dynamite fashions for the spring at a new, lower price point, that are super, super figure-flattering, ladies. So stick around for more fantastic deals, and I'll see you in just a little bit!"

Camera 1 picked up Fanny again.

"We've got a caller on the line, and I'd just love to talk to her right now!" Fanny said. "It's Amaleen from Tennessee—did I get that right?" Thanks for taking the time out of your busy evening to shop with us, Amaleen! How you doing down there in Tennessee?"

"I'm doing great!" Amaleen gushed. "Fanny, you look so beautiful!" No matter how many times Amaleen had called into the show, she never got used to the thrill of talking to her idol.

"Well, Miss Amaleen, thank-you kindly for that compliment. I'm doing great, too. What did we have for you tonight, my friend?"

"I'm ordering the pebble leather pocketbook with the mag-snap closure, Fanny," Amaleen said excitedly.

"Isn't this just a gorgeous bag?" Fanny said, modeling it in the crook of her arm. "It's an absolute must-have this season, don't you think? And by the way, Amaleen, I love that you used the word 'pocketbook'. It's so ladylike, and nowadays it seems like people hardly ever use that word. Right, Amaleen?"

Oh my god, she's asking for my opinion! Amaleen felt light-headed.

"That's right, Fanny! People never say 'pocketbook' anymore, and it's a shame!" Amaleen replied.

I think she remembers me from the other times I've called in! And from my messages and postings on her GHN page! She said I was her 'friend', right out loud on the air!

"You still there, Amaleen?" Fanny asked.

"I sure am, Fanny! And, you know, 'pocketbook' was the word my mother always used, and if it was good enough for her, it sure is good enough for me!"

"I hear you, girlfriend," Fanny replied genially. "I'm kind of an old-fashioned girl myself, and from now on I'm going to be saying 'pocketbook' instead of 'purse'. What do you say we start a new trend, Amaleen, hahaha! A revolution!"

Could it really be? Were they bonding? It was the validation Amaleen had dreamed of.

"Which color did you choose, Miss Amaleen?"

"The blue teal, Fanny," Amaleen replied giddily.

"Oh, that's my favorite color, too!" Fanny said. "It's really pretty, isn't it? I just love that blue teal color—I think it's the new neutral. Goes with absolutely everything. I might just have to order one for myself—unless I can borrow yours, hahaha!"

Fanny's definitely feeling a connection with me! I wonder if this time she's actually going to keep me on the line for a private, personal chat?

"You sure can, Fanny!" Amaleen shouted into the phone. "You can borrow mine anytime you want. Come to think of it, would it be okay if I bought one of these pocketbooks for you, too?"

End the call, the director's voice barked into Fanny's earpiece.

"Well, bless your heart, Amaleen, thank-you so much for calling, and for shopping with us at GHN," Fanny said without missing a beat. "Your beautiful pocketbook will be coming your way in just a few days. Be sure to let us know how much you love it on the GHN website. And please be sure to keep shopping with us. Call anytime! Bye-bye, now!"

Amaleen understood the signals loud and clear. She grasped Fanny's coded message to stay on the line, and clutched the phone to her ear. Her eyes shot around the bedroom at the boxes stacked everywhere. A feeling of sublime contentment washed over her.

The minutes passed, as Amaleen sipped her hot cocoa. She watched Mary Lou Flowers begin the next segment of the show, waiting for Fanny to come back on the line, her stomach fluttering nervously. She suddenly developed the hiccups, and wondered with a giggle if Fanny would tease her about it. Her excitement and anticipation mounted as she held the line.

Five minutes went by. Amaleen's fingers tightened around the phone, and began to cramp. Where was Fanny? Her thoughts began to race. First with confusion. Then, anger. Amaleen began to feel hot. Soon she was damp with sweat. She felt nauseated, and was afraid she was going to throw up. Or faint. She could not be sure how much time passed before she realized that she had been disconnected.

The dead air at the other end of the line roared cruelly in Amaleen's ear. She felt mocked and derided. What now seemed like a pathetic dream of being friends with someone as famous as Fanny Spendlove filled her with a scorching sense of shame. The likes of a woman of Fanny's status was simply out of Amaleen's reach; she should have realized that. How could she have possibly thought otherwise?

Amaleen began to weep. Tears streamed down her face and neck, and splashed onto her rayon, stretch nightie (GHN, $35.50). She tore away the bed cover, and ran to the kitchen through the darkened apartment, trying not to crash into any of the boxes. She thrust her hand blindly into the freezer, and pulled out the first thing she could grab—a box of peanut butter-cheesecake cookies nibbles (two payments of $14.85, GHN). Clutching the ice-cold box to her chest as she ran, she dived back under the covers, and ripped open the cellophane wrapping, sobbing uncontrollably.

Chapter 3

Science cannot solve the ultimate mystery of nature.
And that is because, in the last analysis, we ourselves
are a part of the mystery that we are trying to solve.
~ Max Planck

GHN streamed at a barely audible level in Edwina's office as she worked at the blackboard, fiddling with The Standard Model (of particle physics). The steady prattle from the home shopping network created a veil of white noise that allowed her imagination to wander. She took in none of the actual words emanating from the GHN transmission, but rather, let the chatter provide a buffer against everything but her own thought process.

Along with her fellow supersymmetry theorists around the globe, she hoped to fill in some of the blanks in The Standard Model—the theory that explained the very nature of reality's building blocks. With the ongoing discoveries of new subatomic particles, the rules of the game kept changing, and The Model needed to be expanded; it was currently able to characterize the nature of reality only so far. The work suited Edwina's curious nature. Exploration was for her its own fulfillment.

"And if you happen to be one of the lucky ladies on our next studio tour," an exuberant GHN presenter was saying, "you'll be getting one of these supersized bath gel sets as our way of saying 'thank-you for being a GHN shopper'. And please, please, PLEASE, be sure not to miss GHN's *first ever* saltwater aquarium presentation with Fanny Spendlove, coming up soon! Check your local GHN schedule for this extra-special event!"

The sound of a knock at her door did not register until the third time.

"Come in," Edwina said, looking up.

Paolo Rossetti popped his head inside her office. Edwina smiled, and motioned him in.

"Did you decide what you're going to tell Phil?" Paolo said, closing the door behind him.

"Not yet," she replied. "I'm still thinking about it. Haven't really decided how I feel about it."

"Oh? Phil Kimby asks you to meet with him about joining his quantum team at the NSA, and you don't jump at the opportunity? Rising stars must expect such things, you know," Paolo chided.

Edwina sat down next to him on the sofa, tucking her legs underneath her. A pair of jeans and a pale, flowery shirt clad her slender figure, and she looked more like a graduate student than an assistant professor. Chin length hair showed off her long neck, and framed a heart-shaped face.

"I'm not sure what the point would be," she said. "What purpose does it serve if my work on entanglement and superposition ends up helping the government spy on more people, more efficiently?"

"What about the rest of it?" Paolo said, "The real point of the work? The part where your contribution to quantum cryptology helps stop extremists and lunatics from communicating freely over the internet in order to organize future terrorist attacks?"

Edwina flicked her long bangs to the side in a familiar gesture, and gazed out the window. A companionable silence fell over the office.

"I've been thinking a lot about how Einstein regretted writing that letter to Roosevelt in '39," she said, "urging him to develop atomic weaponry. Once our government perfects this new generation of technological capability," she continued, "other governments will develop it too, and heaven knows what they'll use it for—all sorts of nefarious things! Theoretically, governments could use it to track the gender of unborn babies if they want, and decide which mothers are allowed to go to full term! It makes me feel slightly sick when I think about all the possible applications of the work Phil wants me for at the NSA."

Paolo regarded his younger colleague sympathetically as she gazed pensively out the window. A gust of wind caused the branches of a nearby tree to bob up and down, creaking.

"No; I don't think I'll accept Phil's offer," she said. "I don't want my work to become part of anything like that."

"Your feelings and concerns are understandable," Paolo said. "And yet, we know quantum computer technology is already here, and there's no way to stop its advancement. I wonder—are you quite certain you don't want to be part of the team that puts this new cryptology on the map? By the way, Edwina, what does your handsome detective think?"

She looked at Paolo quizzically.

"I haven't mentioned it to him," she said.

"Why is that?" Paolo said.

"No particular reason," she shrugged. "It's *my* decision, not his."

Paolo glanced at his watch, and stood up to leave.

"I have to go and meet with a student," he said. "But, I'm curious—don't you trust Will?"

"Of course I do."

"Well, then," Paolo said, "lower the drawbridge. Nobody likes being shut out of the conversation, Edwina. Especially by someone they care for. I know you don't mean to be, but try not to be such an island."

***

Donald Gaylord tended his grapevine with all the care and devotion of the most committed of gardeners, and it didn't take long for news of Edwina's NSA offer to reach him.

His first thought was that it must be a mistake—that it had been meant for him, and somehow wires had gotten crossed. But, as the authenticity of the news trickled in, he experienced it as a rejection so egregious, so stinging, that for two and a half days his blood pressure spiked dangerously, and he did not sleep.

Chapter 4

*The goal of life is to make your heartbeat match the
beat of the universe, to match your nature with Nature.*
~ Joseph Campbell

The cottage on Trotter Farm Road where Edwina
lived had been built in 1927 for the foreman of Trotter
Farm, a thriving, New England dairy in those days. She
had lived there since the second year of her
undergraduate days, and made the commute to campus
on her bike in ten minutes or so. She rented the cottage
from Francis Trotter, whose family still owned the
farm, and all the land on Trotter Farm Road, including
the original farmhouse down the way. Quiet and
bucolic, it was the only privately owned street
remaining in New Guilford.

These days, Francis Trotter lived at The Willows, an
assisted living place in town. His daughter, Daisy, lived
with her husband, Joe, and their children in the old
farmhouse, a rambling clapboard affair just down the
road from Edwina's cottage. Daisy and Joe were
devoted to the old farm. They kept a large vegetable
garden, chickens, a few goats, and honey bees. Joe
worked in finance, but mostly thought of himself as a
farmer. In the summer and fall months Daisy and Joe
sold their goods at the farmer's market in town. Their
two older children, now in middle-school, did not share
their parents' enthusiasm for the pastoral lifestyle, but
Jane, the youngest (10), was passionate about the farm.
She had set her sights on a career in the agrisciences,
and dreamed of turning the place back into a working

farm someday, and adding lots of animals. Admiring of Edwina as a fellow scientist, Jane occasionally left things for her at the cottage—fresh eggs; a jar of wildflower honey; a bunch of flowers. If Edwina happened to be home, she usually invited Jane inside for a visit and a cup of tea.

The kitchen had become the largest room in Edwina's two story cottage when the walls separating the kitchen from the original dining room were removed years earlier. A handsome, cast iron wood stove now stood in the middle of the kitchen. The heart of the cottage, it ably heated the whole house. With a string of winters under her belt on Trotter's Farm Road, Edwina had become a dab hand at keeping the wood-burning stove stoked.

She graded papers at the kitchen table as Will cooked dinner. Streaming at a low volume in the background, a GHN host was demonstrating an oversized, outdoor chess set. Twenty-inch tall plastic game pieces stood on a ten foot square, all-weather game board made of vinyl. The whole set was illuminated, as demonstrated by the dimmed lights in the GHN studio.

"Hey, Will," Edwina said. "Check this out. Bet you've never seen one of these, before."

"At this price point," an enthusiastic presenter said, "you've got to be asking yourself, 'how can *I not* pick up this beautiful, outdoor checkers and chess set? Heck, why not get one for yourself, *and* one as a gift for that special son or niece or grandchild? Stock up for the holidays! I know I'm going to! Think about all the fun you're missing out on—how exciting would it be to play outside with the entire family? And the whole thing lights up, so you can even enjoy playing at nighttime! Wouldn't this just make the most unique gift, ever?"

She demonstrated how light weight the game pieces were by picking up a King's pawn with two fingers.

"Checkmate, hahaha!" the fun-loving presenter exclaimed. "Gee, why do I feel like Alice in Wonderland all of a sudden! Seriously, the entire set is light as a feather. And, it's a snap to put away. It comes with this set of sturdy, nylon carrying cases—your choice of blue and white stripes, or holiday red. The game board itself is fabricated from a super light vinyl that rolls up easily for quick storage. We'll even include the batteries for the LED lighting, if you call in now. That's quite a savings! You won't find this incredible item anywhere else, folks. It was made especially for GHN. Just think how jealous your neighbors will be!"

***

After dinner, Edwina ran a bath, and reviewed her earlier conversation with Paolo. Feelings of guilt mounted over not having shared the NSA news with Will. She tried to put it out of her mind, and focused instead on the crossword puzzle in her hand.

"Hey, Will?" she called through the open door. "What's a four letter word that means, 'emasculated Pinocchio'?"

"What?" he replied from the hallway, a putty knife poised in his hand, piled with spackle compound.

"Oops," Edwina said. "Never mind—it's 'emulated Pinocchio', not 'emasculated'!"

"Lied," Will said from the hallway.

When Edwina emerged from the bathroom a short time later, it was with a towel wrapped snugly around her, and combed-out, wet hair.

"That looks great, Will," she said, bending down to peer at his handiwork. "Can't even tell there was a gouge there."

"When it dries I'll give it a good sanding and a fresh coat of paint," he said, wiping the putty knife off with a rag.

"What would you think of painting the door a different color?" she said. "Maybe bright blue or something?"

Will glanced up and down the small upstairs hallway at the cream-colored doors and walls.

"Huh. Could be," he said tactfully. "I'll pick up some paint samples."

Edwina turned to face him. Her wet bangs fell over anxious, wide set, hazel-gray eyes. Will breathed in her sweet, soapy smell, but could not read her expression. Droplets of water fell from the ends of her hair, and landed on the hallway runner in muffled 'plops'.

"What's up?" he said.

"The NSA," she blurted out.

"I'm sorry?" Will said. "What?"

"It's my work. An old colleague asked me to join his quantum cryptography project—cyber security stuff. It would mean working in Maryland once in a while, and getting all sorts of clearances. But I decided I'm not going to do it. It's really been on my mind, and I'm sorry I didn't tell you about it."

Will regarded her evenly.

"Why was that?" he said.

They stood in an awkward silence in the little hallway.

Will spoke after a few moments.

"Look. First of all, congratulations about the NSA thing. That's a huge deal, Edwina. Second, I guess we can't help being the way we are. We're both used to living alone—used to keeping our own counsel. But going forward, maybe we can practice keeping each other in the loop. What do you think?"

***

Will gazed up at the framed, periodic poster on the wall of Edwina's bedroom as they lay in bed. The moon cast a frosty beam of light into the darkened room.

"Your turn," he said.

"Hm," Edwina muttered. "So it is. Let's see. 'Prism'," she said. "'Pr' for *praseodymium*; 'I' for *iodine*; and 'Sm' for *samarium*."

Edwina ran her fingers through Will's hair as he studied the chart, searching for another word to piece together out of the lettered symbols in brightly colored squares.

"Heat," he said. "'He' for helium; 'At' for astatine. 'Heat'."

"Very nice," Edwina said. "Short, but acceptable."

"Your go," Will said, stretching sleepily.

"Pouncer!" she said after some moments. "'Po' for polonium; 'U' for uranium; 'N' for nitrogen; 'C' for carbon; and 'Er' for erbium."

"Very impressive," Will yawned.

The house was quiet. The only sound came from the occasional acorn falling onto the roof, and rolling its way down the dormer gables.

"You know, I've always meant to ask—why is it you have a periodic chart on the wall?" Will said.

"Because it's so beautiful," she said. "Just look at it! The first time I saw one was in fifth grade. Miss Battersby showed it to our class. She talked about it for a long time, and when I finally grasped that all those little boxes with their mysterious symbols and numbers and colors represented the elements in the universe— and that they were arranged according to protons in their nuclei, and increasing atomic weights—I fainted."

"You fainted in class?" Will said.

"Yeah, I hyperventilated, and blacked out. Chipped a tooth on my desk, and everything. I was blown away that someone had figured out how to arrange all the known elements of the universe in such beautiful order. It was like a map of life."

Edwina lay in Will's arms and peered out the window. The planets and stars twinkled and winked at her. Will was drifting off to sleep. She began to picture faraway stars, exploding and imploding silently (there is no sound in space)—their fireworks producing all the nitrogen in our DNA, every atom in our bodies. She imagined a kilanova—a massive collision of two neutron stars—a merger so magnificent that the impact created an eruption of gold dust. The cores of these neutron clusters, known as 'nuclear pasta', were thought to be the toughest material in the known universe.

She propped herself up on one elbow, and peered at Will in the moonlight. As she ran her eyes slowly over the planes and contours of his face, she contemplated the nature of the current that ran between them. What did this invisible force consist of? Could its properties be parsed and measured, like electricity or gravity or magnetism? Was it possible to take the measure of the thing that connected them?

Poets and painters had tried to describe love for centuries. Why not physicists and mathematicians? Maybe scientists would be the ones to explain matters of the heart. Perhaps love and desire could be measured by an algorithm factoring in pheromones, brain peptides, chemical messaging systems between neurons, and human electrical units.

She lay back on the pillow, and closed her eyes. Life was not much more than a spark bookended by darkness, but it was full of the most exhilarating things. Like the nuclear pasta inside neutron stars, and the warm smell of Will.

Chapter 5

Be careful what you set your heart upon—for it will surely be yours.
~ James Baldwin

Connie Biggs arrived bright and early at the post office, the very first customer that day.

"Hey, Cousin Honey," she said to her friend behind the counter.

"Hey, Connie," Amaleen replied.

"Guess why I don't have any packages or nothing?"

The last thing Amaleen felt like that morning was playing guessing games. Connie was her best friend, but Amaleen was still licking her wounds from the other night's humiliation over the thwarted encounter with Fanny Spendlove on the phone. Amaleen regarded Connie with some annoyance.

"I don't know what you're talking about," Amaleen said. "And what are you grinning at, anyway? You look like a donkey in a briar patch; you know that? You look foolish, is what."

"Don't you even want to guess?" Connie said cheerfully.

"Not really," Amaleen said. "Better just spit out whatever you've got stuck in your craw."

"You know what, Cousin Honey?" Not even one of your stinky moods is gonna' bother me today," Connie chuckled. "Not today! You know that contest we entered a few months ago? For the GHN trip?"

Amaleen stared at Connie mutely.

"Can you even believe it?" Connie said. "That's right; you're looking directly at the winner! Get your bags packed, 'cause New Hampshire, here we come!"

The women had promised they would take the other along if one of them were to win the all-expenses paid, weekend trip to the GHN studios. They had been talking about it for months, even praying that one of them would win. The prize included airfare, hotel, transportation to and from the airport, and a limo back and forth from the hotel to GHN. Not to mention, a 50% off gift certificate for any GHN purchase.

Connie Biggs prattled on about a few items that had caught her eye, to use with that gift certificate, and asked Amaleen's advice about which one she should choose, but Amaleen was preoccupied, and slow to respond. Amaleen could not let Connie know the reason her feelings about their dream trip to GHN had cooled. It would be so humiliating if Connie ever found out what had happened the other night, when Amaleen had called GHN, purchased a handbag, waited for a private conversation with Fanny Spendlove, and then suffered the indignity of being hung up on while she had been filled with such hopeful excitement. Her dream of becoming friends with Fanny Spendlove had been mercilessly dashed, and a trip to GHN seemed like rubbing salt in the wound. Amaleen would never hear the end of it if she confided in Connie. She tried to come up with an excuse for not going, but she could think of no way to back out of the trip. She would have to go. Her stomach knotted up at the thought.

Connie was still trying to get Amaleen's advice about whether to use her 50% GHN discount on the splashing-birds-rechargeable-solar-powered   fountain, or the superior-suction-self-regulating-robot-vacuum cleaner, which would be the more practical item.

Amaleen did her best to express enthusiasm for the solar fountain, and Connie agreed.

"In your heart, I think the fountain's what you really want," Amaleen said.

A gut bomb of dread had begun to grow in Amaleen. She glanced at the clock. The minutes were going by tortuously slowly. She begrudgingly forced herself to think about what clothes she would need to pack for their trip. When she got home she would look for the suitcase she had bought a few years back from GHN, a very pretty piece of luggage with fancy, logo-lined interior compartments, 360 degree spinner wheels, and a retractable handle. She had picked it up for three convenient payments of only $21.99, but hadn't had the occasion to use it, yet, since she never traveled. She tried to cheer herself up by imagining what an impressive figure she would cut at the airport, sporting her recently purchased, teal handbag, all dressed up, toting this brand new piece of designer luggage behind her. Its purchase had been the cause of much excitement for Amaleen at the time, imagining that maybe she would start doing some traveling, and see the world. But when it came right down to it, she had no real desire to leave Crawford. Now, she would have to.

People say some of the best moments in life are the unplanned ones, and that when one door closes, another one opens unexpectedly. When, on an impulse (or was it intuition?) Amaleen decided to answer a phone call from an unidentified caller on her way home from the post office that evening–something she would not ordinarily do—that is exactly what happened. The phone call opened a door, and a ray of hope shone on her.

Things were starting to look up.

Chapter 6

The first step in the evolution of ethics is a sense of
solidarity with other human beings.
~ Albert Schweitzer

On her way into the kitchen to get more ice, Mary Lou Flowers stumbled, and fell against the life-sized, promotional poster of herself hanging in the hallway of her condominium apartment. Its heavy frame shuddered against the wall, but did not come crashing down from the hook. The heavily air-brushed photo portrait showed her standing on one of the earliest GHN sets, smiling, her arms outstretched to showcase a display of beauty products. A former Miss Delaware beauty contest winner, Mary Lou had been the original face of the GHN Network when it opened for business decades earlier.

It had been a good run as Queen Bee of the hive. She held the record at GHN for being the most successful presenter in the history of the network, a statistic calculated in terms of dollars earned per on-air minutes in a single show. Mary Lou remained the favorite host of thousands of loyal viewers, and she still received fan letters every week (although not as many as she once did) asking for advice on everything from make-up tips to recipes to marital problems. With a growing awareness that her reign was on the downhill slide, Mary Lou seized every opportunity to maximize the remainder of her minor celebrity status. She agreed to any and every request for personal appearances, whether it was cutting the ribbon at the opening of a new bowling lane, or having a sandwich named after her at the local deli, or christening a new fire truck. Attention was attention, after all.

But, time is stubborn; it only travels in one direction, and age was a touchy subject for Mary Lou Flowers. Although there was no officially stated retirement age at GHN, the general feeling was that the magic number hovered around sixty, and Mary Lou would be fifty-six on her next birthday. That made her one of the older presenters at the network—still popular, but far from the heady, early days when she was the undisputed star at GHN. Younger hosts had showed up with their fashionable haircuts, and trendy fashion sense—the 'relatability factor' was how the executives described it—and it was not only expected of Mary Lou to be a gracious, team player, but to be a supportive booster of all these threatening newcomers. Chief among them was Fanny Spendlove, an ambitious dynamo whom Mary Lou was certain had set her cap at becoming GHN's new queen. Fanny was instantly popular with viewers, and grew more so by the month. Mary Lou checked Fanny's GHN page obsessively to see how many fans had posted comments lauding her.

With all of this very much on her mind, Mary Lou lay sprawled on the living room sofa in a state somewhere between stupefaction and oblivion, a large tumbler of gin and Dubonnet balanced precariously on her soft belly. Dressed in a voluminous, rhinestone-embellished kaftan (GHN $49.50), she stared glassy-eyed at the television. Tears streamed down her face as she watched *All About Eve*, projecting her own tragic predicament onto Bette Davis's portrayal of an aging stage actress whose popularity and success is gradually displaced by a scheming, young upstart.

Initially when Fanny had arrived at GHN she had come to Mary Lou frequently for advice and tips. Even though Mary Lou did take pleasure from lauding her senior standing over the novice, had she realized what an ambitious ingrate Fanny would turn out to be, she never would have been so generous with her time in the first place. Fanny had been virtually clueless about things like what colors to avoid wearing on air (white; too glaring), and how to make your sales pitch sound like an over-the-backyard-fence-conversation instead of a hard sell (avoid negative terms like 'hassle-free'; it suggests a hassle factor), and so on.

Mary Lou took a gulp of her drink. Still lying on her back, she raised one arm in the air, and floated it above her. She rotated and examined her hand slowly, as if it were an alien specimen.

Goddamned liver spots!

Body make-up could only do so much to cover the brown blotches, and the thin, blue veins in her once milky hands. Mary Lou wept bitterly at her fate, spurred on by the backdrop of Margo Channing's cruel and unfeeling victimization at the hands of the scheming Eve Harrington.

Mary Lou fixed herself another drink, and exhorted herself to get a grip. What good would it do to cry over spilt milk? She still looked darned good, she reminded herself, regardless of the slings and arrows she had suffered lately during the mandatory review sessions with her bosses at GHN. During a recent review of one of her segments, she had caught the looks passing between the male execs when the camera happened to catch Mary Lou from an unflattering angle. Surely, that was the cameraman's fault, not hers! She would have to speak to him about it. So what if she carried a few extra pounds, anyway? A lot of women did! Didn't she work out at the gym four days a week? And, like any good soldier in the beauty wars, didn't she avail herself of every possible treatment in order to valiantly fight fine lines and wrinkles, restore collagen, and firm her sagging jaw line?

She took another gulp from her glass.

Bastards are lucky to have me! I'd like to see them drag their fat-assed cheap suits in front of the cameras and try to sell some of the junk we peddle. That'd be a laugh! I would kill to see how many units of that new line of cheesy men's shapewear they could unload!

On the heels of this spirited but short-lived rally, Mary Lou fell back into a gin soaked agony of self-pity. She knew when her time was up at GHN and she was off the air, she would fade from the hearts and minds of her fans. She would become just another overweight, middle-aged woman, with too much plastic surgery, and too little money in the bank. In an acrimonious divorce settlement her ex-husband had laid claim to half of her GHN salary. Soon enough, money would become a serious worry for her.

Mary Lou switched from the movie channel back to GHN. Dora Lawrence was presenting a set of "jewel" clad, stacking bracelets with interlocking cross embellishments. Dora was wearing a Sue Shamrack pants suit whose cheerful lime green polka dots did little to distract from an unflattering fit.

"These bracelets are just, plain inspirational," Dora said. "They are the absolute, perfect gift for that church-going Christian on your gift list, because they have such a—*spiritual* quality when you put them on. You instantly feel uplifted. Maybe it's your mom, or your sister, or your daughter, or grandma. Whoever it is, I hope you'll go ahead and purchase a set of these gorgeous bracelets for yourself, as well. You deserve them, ladies! You know I'm right about that!"

Mary Lou raised her head up off the sofa, and addressed the television.

"Hey, Dora—didn't you get the memo? Pants suits make your thighs look about fifty times bigger," she hissed drunkenly. "Seriously? Did you even bother to look in the frigging mirror before you went on the air? Big mistake, Dora. Polka dots are not your color!"

Lately, it seemed, hurling lively abuse at her on-air colleagues eased Mary Lou's burdens. It made her feel positively *alive*.

"Trust me, girlfriend, you could stand to lose a few!" Mary Lou cackled. "And by the way, what's going on with your hair? Looks like a raccoon took a frigging dump up there."

Mary Lou's head fell back against the cushion. She gazed mawkishly around her living room, and found herself moved to tears, once again. She wept over the beauty and refinement of her own, elegant taste. A pair of bronzed, angel figurine lamps ($49.00 and change GHN) sat atop a lightly distressed oak-veneer console table (two flex payments of $57.95). Next to the console was a Lazy Boy recliner, handsomely upholstered in a merlot vinyl fabric that matched the sectional sofa. A trio of delicately hand-painted ceramic cows, lit up by an automatic timer, perched cheerfully on the window sill.

"F-fat cow!" Mary Lou muttered, turning her attention back to Dora Lawrence.

Mary Lou began to moo. Her long, drawn-out bovine utterances grew louder and longer, until an uncontrollable bout of laughter unleashed her bladder. Now wet and uncomfortable, she was further startled by the ringing phone, and when she reached across the coffee table to answer it, she became tangled up in her kaftan, and knocked over her glass. Gin and ice splattered everywhere, and dribbled onto the carpet from the table.

"Hul-lo?" she slurred into the phone.

"It's me," a man's voice replied.

These two simple words stirred in Mary Lou a sudden fury.

"Oh, yeah?" she said. "Well, what about *me*? You ever think of that? How about leaving that bitch like you keep promising—ever think of that?"

Mary Lou was not so drunk that she did not instantly regret saying these things. She clutched the phone tightly, and hoped he would not hang up on her. Maybe he would think she was just joking around.

"Not again," muttered the weary voice of GHN Vice-President of Marketing, Brad Pilfer.

"How much have you had tonight?" he said. "How about putting the bottle away, Mary Lou? You're on the air tomorrow, and you're not doing yourself any favors, you know. You look puffy enough as it is, and you're already skating on pretty thin ice at the network."

"It's only a teensy bit of gin with mostly ice and Dubonnet," she whined. "Same exact thing the Queen of England drinks, for Chrissakes! You coming over, baby?"

Silence.

"Brad, are you there?"

By anyone's measure, theirs was not a relationship made in heaven, or anywhere in its celestial environs. VP Brad Pilfer, had, indeed, hung up on her.

The fact that Brad had a wife and children had not deterred Mary Lou from initiating an affair with him (nor had it deterred him), which she did solely based on Brad's intense dislike of Fanny Spendlove. It was a quality Mary Lou found arousing, perhaps his only such quality. She wasn't sure why he hated Fanny, and she didn't care; all she knew was that Brad's antipathy toward her arch rival made him very desirable. Their Fanny-bashing sessions did much to ease Mary Lou's anxiety and jealousy.

Fuming mad at her spineless lover boy for hanging up on her, Mary Lou blearily scrolled through the photos on her phone until she came to the one she was looking for: a bare-bottomed, hirsute Brad, sprawled on top of her. In fact, passed out. They had both had too much to drink on that particular occasion, but with his head turned to the side, his face was still clearly recognizable. The photo was, of course, her secret insurance policy.

Mary Lou did some fuzzy, mental calculus. She figured if Brad left his wife, and married her, her job at GHN would be protected. She deeply resented the eventuality of being put out to pasture, and her forced retirement was feeling increasingly imminent after Brad's remark about 'thin ice'. Surely marrying Brad would give her some built-in security and maybe even a bit of clout?

She told herself she had better sober up before she came to any decision about sending the photo to Brad's wife, which in Mary Lou's mind, would start the ball rolling toward a favorable outcome for herself. Some people are observed to become a different person when they drink, which explained the fact that Mary Lou #1 (sober/cautious) and Mary Lou #2 (drunk/impulsive) were engaged in a spirited disagreement over whether or not to send the incriminating photo to Mrs. Pilfer. Mary Lou #2 won the argument with a click of the phone.

How thrilling it was, she thought, staring at the phone, waiting excitedly for some sort of response that was about to change her life. Mary Lou had a special talent for seeing her own, morally questionable behavior as righteous, as if she were seeing it through a prism forged in crazy town that refracted bad behavior into looking like virtue. After all, she told herself, didn't she deserve to be happy? In her current frame of mind she was hurting, and didn't that give her every right to find solace and comfort however she could? Mary Lou was nothing less than a moral alchemist who could turn wrong into right, and accountability into blame.

She passed out on the sofa in her damp kaftan into a fitful sleep, where the veil of rationalization evaporated, and without it, her mind was laid bare to an unforgiving conscience. Maybe it was the excessive alcohol consumption that made her toss and turn so much. Or maybe somewhere deep down inside she knew there was something not right about sleeping with a married man, or having to stupefy her senses with alcohol on a nightly basis in order to justify it. Was there possibly a better version of herself floating around somewhere, wanting to make itself known? She dreamed about Fanny Spendlove and Brad. They were laughing at her as they made love on the indoor/outdoor recliner Mary Lou had presented earlier in the week for three convenient payments of $169.98. The dream seemed to go on for a very long time, and nothing would allow her a good night's sleep. After all, even a seasoned saleswoman like Mary Lou could only sell so much fertilizer, especially to herself.

The compromising photograph of her husband caused terrible consternation and pain when Mrs. Pilfer received the text, but after a twenty-four hour turnaround, as forgiving and pious-minded as she was, Martha Pilfer found her way to forgive her wayward husband, and decided to give him another chance, for the sake of the children. In return, Brad Pilfer was so grateful for his wife's kindness, he promised to redouble his efforts at marital fidelity.

Chapter 7

The universe is not required to be in perfect harmony
with human ambition.
~ Carl Sagan

Fanny Spendlove inspected the unpleasant visage looking back at her from the mirror. Smudged mascara cartoonishly underlined blood shot eyes and puffy lids. Her whole face looked swollen, even her nose. A mournful whimper escaped through her parched lips. Too little sleep, too much alcohol consumption, once again.

She stepped into the shower with a kind of tentative, slow-motion movement, trying to avoid any sudden eruption from her queasy stomach. She stood under the hot water and let the pelting spray massage her throbbing head until the pain in her scalp and neck began to ease up. Her head bowed, she gave a silent shout-out of gratitude to the inventor of the adjustable-three-speed-jet-spray-showerhead (two payments of under $69.50). It was taking the edge off her hangover.

Fanny stepped out of the shower, and regarded herself once again in the mirror, an apricot-colored towel wrapped in a turban around her head, and a terry robe belted loosely around her waist. Feeling somewhat better, she began to shift her weight from one foot to the other, like a boxer. Rolling her shoulders and raising her fists she began throwing jabs and uppercuts at the mirror.

"Time to get to work, champ!" she said.

***

On the drive to GHN, Fanny felt her confidence coursing back through her body as she psyched herself up to get on the air that day and sell, sell, sell! Nowhere did she feel more exhilarated than under the demanding conditions of live television, where she could see sales being tracked by the minute on a digital read-out screen, and segment producers barked instructions and updates into her earpiece in real time.

"Bring it on!" she muttered under her breath as she strode across the parking lot toward Studio B, anxious to get into hair and make-up. She was looking especially ashen and bloodshot that morning.

She grabbed the notes for her show on the way into the makeup room. As soon as she plopped down into the chair, Esther Rubenstein began to flutter around her, brandishing make-up brushes and sponges. William Wyler's 1939 *Wuthering Heights* was streaming on the flat screen.

"Heathcliff, don't break my heart," Merle Oberon said.

"Oh Cathy, I never broke your heart," replied Laurence Olivier. "You broke it! Cathy! Cathy! You loved me! What right to throw love away for the poor fancy thing you felt for him, for a handful of worldliness . . ."

"What the hell's that you've got on, Esther?" Fanny said. "What's 'a handful of worldliness' supposed to mean? What is this, Shakespeare?"

"Judging from the tone of your voice, I'm thinking that was a rhetorical question," Esther said icily, "but I'm going to answer it, anyway. The things you younger people don't know! Haven't you heard of *Wuthering Heights*? It's only one of the greatest, tragic love stories of all time."

"Nope."

"Ever heard the name Emily Bronte?" Esther said.

"Should I?" Fanny replied.

Esther let out an exasperated sigh.

"Heathcliff and Cathy have been soul mates since they were kids. They've been like one person. Heathcliff's angry at Cathy for squandering the deep love they've had for each other all their lives, and for deciding to marry Edgar Linton instead, because she thinks she wants the conventional life of money and social standing and worldly goods that Linton can give her. She chooses a life with Linton instead of a life of true happiness with Heathcliff."

"Oh, for Chrissake, Esther, would you mute it?" Fanny said.

Esther snatched up the remote control, and killed the sound.

"You're crankier than usual today. Late night again?" Esther said.

"What gave it away?" Fanny said. "The dark circles, the bloodshot eyes, or the smell of margaritas coming out of my pores? Listen, Esther," Fanny said as Esther put hot curlers into her hair. "Would you mind running down to the cafeteria? I didn't have time to eat this morning. Grab me some scrambled eggs, bacon, buttered toast, and a latte. Got a big show today. Thanks."

Full of resentment, Esther put the last curler in Fanny's hair. She glanced over at a shelf crammed with vitamins, supplements, and homeopathic remedies, and fantasized about putting a crazy concoction of something in Fanny's latte, just to teach her a lesson about manners.

"Sure," Esther said, "but you shouldn't be eating so much cholesterol and fat, you know. You should do like I keep telling you, and get on a solid regimen of vitamins. For starters, you should be taking this stuff," she said, shaking a bottle of biotin capsules in front of Fanny's face.

"It'd really help thicken up your hair, you know."

Esther shoved the bottle of capsules into her pocket. She had learned not to expect much in the way of politeness from Fanny Spendlove, but Fanny's behavior that morning had lowered the bar considerably. She stewed all the way to the cafeteria.

Who the heck does she think she is, anyway? How could anyone be so completely oblivious to somebody else's feelings? What a brat!

Absently fingering the bottle of vitamin capsules in her pocket on the way to the cafeteria, Esther turned her mind to her days as a young actress, living and working in New York. Along the way, she had fallen in love, and married a young actor. Life was full of promise, then. These memories constituted the happiest time of her life, but now it seemed as if they existed in a parallel world in some remote dimension, so far away, barely even real. She found it difficult to reconcile the world of her past with her current life, where she had to deal with abusive philistines like Fanny Spendlove, instead of the clever and amusing theater people who once filled her life. Esther's handsome, young (ex)husband had grown old and cynical, and no longer resembled the romantic hero of her youth. She wondered if he ever reminisced about the genteel landscape of their youth. She longed for the days when the people around her seemed to have more in the way of substance, and when good manners were *de riguer*.

Oh, Esther, don't be such a sap, she thought, tearing herself from this sentimental reverie. *You're just feeling sorry for yourself. Did you forget, it wasn't too much fun not having any money back then!*

When she returned to the makeup room, and placed the breakfast tray on Fanny's lap, she received only a brief nod of thanks. Fanny wasted no time digging in.

"Don't mention it," Esther said under her breath.

Ever the professional, she went about her job with her usual efficiency and aplomb, applying Fanny's makeup, and styling her hair, making her look as attractive as humanly possible, and using every available weapon in her arsenal to do it. She used twelve different products for Fanny's eyes alone—a serum for under eye puffiness; a primer to hold the color; a base layer of color corrector; concealer paste; eye shadow primer; eye shadow cream; eyeliner; brow pencil; false lashes; brow highlighter; setting powder, and fixing spray. Serious makeup application was not for the faint-hearted.

***

"Hello!" Fanny gushed into camera one. "Welcome to the show, my lovely shoppers, and thanks so much for joining me today! And a super-duper special welcome to our group of lucky contest winners who got to take a tour of the studio here at GHN!"

Amaleen returned to her seat from the ladies' room just in time for the start of the show. Connie Biggs nudged her in the side, and Amaleen shot her a withering look.

"Sorry, Cousin Honey!" Connie whispered. "I didn't mean to poke you so hard. I can't believe we're actually here! Isn't this exciting? Look how beautiful Fanny is in person!"

"You think so?" Amaleen whispered. "She looks a little rode hard and put up wet to me. She looks a lot older than I thought she would."

"Thank-you all so much for being with me here at GHN for some super fun shopping!" Fanny said. "Today I have the great pleasure of presenting one of the most amazing, amazing items we've ever had the privilege to offer, and I cannot wait to get started, so let's get shopping! Say it with me, now, ladies!" The studio audience couldn't have been more obliging, as they merrily chanted,

Stores with doors, oh, what bores!

The set design for Fanny's presentation was done in an undersea theme. The backdrop featured a vintage-style illustration of a mermaid and a walrus frolicking in the ocean, next to an outcropping of rocks. Green and blue glass globes the size of beach balls hung from overhead in fishermen's netting, along with oversized starfish. Fanny was dressed in a strapless, metallic turquoise gown with a mermaid style silhouette that flared at the bottom. Despite various items of heavily elasticized shape wear, she moved with agility and ease around the set.

"GHN has given me the honor of presenting a very special product for the first time ever. We have already received 800 advance orders for this amazing item," she said, putting her hands together in prayer fashion, telegraphing some sort of religious experience.

"What we have for you today, my friends, is a sixty-five gallon saltwater aquarium. You probably never thought you could own one of these incredible tanks, but the fact is, that GHN partnered with modern technology and a team of cutting-edge designers to make saltwater fish-keeping easier than ever before!"

"Let's start right here," she said, "with this amazing algae magnet cleaner. It automatically keeps the tank clean, so you don't have to slave over it, and do all that scrubbing and scraping. And, this one-step salt mix makes changing the tank water easier than ever. Heck! In the old days you actually had to trek to the beach to replace the salt water, but not anymore!"

"As you can see, the tank also comes with this gorgeous pine and birch veneer stand, and this fabulous matching canopy, which is just so pretty. These designer doors open up into a very roomy cabinet, so you can store all of your cleaning items inside. Super convenient," she said, gliding around effortlessly in four inch heels.

"Now, I need you to know that this aquarium is made of acrylic, which is actually seventeen times stronger than glass, not to mention it'll never break like glass—just one more thing you never have to worry about," Fanny said. "You get your choice of background panels—sapphire blue, black, or clear. The aquarium will arrive to you fully outfitted and assembled, with a light, and automatic timer, this carbon filter, this skimmer, your algae magnet cleaner, and a supply of one-step salt mix. Isn't that *amazing*? GHN has thought of everything!"

"But I haven't even gotten to the best part!" she said. "GHN worked out a special offer with our vendor to include with your purchase a set of free starter fish! You will receive live coral—which actually helps to keep the tank naturally fresh and clean—and three adorable saltwater fish, just like these cute little guys! You also receive an instruction booklet, and the free info hotline for any questions you might have about looking after your tank."

"Sales are spiking. Stay on the live fish," the voice from the control room said in Fanny's earpiece.

"Now, this special offer including the free fish ends at midnight, tonight, so please don't wait, if you're on the fence," Fanny said. "If you order the aquarium *after* midnight, you'll receive three *dead* fish, hahahaha! I'm just kidding about that, but seriously, saltwater fish are not cheap, so this really is a tremendous deal—a once in a lifetime offer—and I do *not* want you to miss out on it! Just look how amazing these little guys are!"

Fanny moved around the set, opening and closing cabinet doors, raising and lowering the little canopy, feeding the fish, her steady patter never faltering.

"Can you just imagine how excited your kids would be to see this fabulous aquarium in your family room on Christmas morning? Or, how about your retired parents, who might be getting a little older, and maybe they don't get out quite as much? How perfect would this be? Entertainment *and* companionship! I'll tell you what—whoever said 'less is more' sure as heck never shopped at GHN! I say 'more is more'—am I right, hahahaha? This gorgeous, easy care aquarium is the proof! Life is short, folks; grab it while you can! Who says you can't have it all!"

Fanny was hitting it out of the park. She had the audience in the palm of her hand, as sales mounted. Connie Biggs laughed and clapped appreciatively at Fanny's jokes, along with the rest of the studio audience.

"Take a call," said the voice in Fanny's earpiece.

"Hey, guys, it's time for a caller," Fanny said, "and we've got Betsy from Baton Rouge. Hey, Bets!"

"Hi, Fanny," the caller said. "Thanks for taking my call. I watch you all the time. You're my favorite host."

"Thanks so much!" Fanny said. "I really appreciate that! What do you think of this amazing aquarium, Miss Betsy?"

"I think it's beautiful, Fanny. I'm getting it for my husband. He's been wanting an aquarium for his office for quite a while, and I just couldn't believe it when I saw this one on GHN."

"Wow, that's great!" Fanny replied. "I'm so thrilled we have it for you, Betsy! What kind of work does your husband do down there in Louisiana?"

"He's a criminal prosecutor," Betsy said.

"Whoa!" Fanny said, raising her hands in the air. "I'm innocent, I swear, hahahaha! I'm just kidding with you, Betsy."

"Hahahaha!" Betsy laughed. "Fanny, could I just say that I've been shopping at GHN for many years, and I think you're just great—so down to earth and authentic!"

Fanny struck an 'aw-shucks-I-don't-deserve-it'-pose—hands on hips, head cocked to one side, an exaggerated, mock frowny-face expression.

"You just made my whole day, you know that, Betsy?" Fanny said. "Heck, you made my whole month! Thanks very much for your kind words. I sure appreciate it! This job wouldn't mean a darn thing without nice folks like you to talk to."

"Now, we'll be getting this aquarium right out to you, Betsy. You should have it in about a week. It's going to come outfitted with all the amazing extras you see here—the gorgeous wood stand and cabinet, the adorable canopy, the light and automatic timer, the carbon filter, skimmer, salt water mix, and algae cleaner."

"And the fish?" Betsy asked.

"Yes, ma'am!" Fanny said. "And I'll make sure none of these little rascals has a criminal record, cuz' I'd hate to see your husband have to put one of them in fish jail! Hahahaha! You'll be receiving three healthy saltwater fish—fingers crossed there's no piranhas in there, hahahaha—and your live coral, too. Which background color did you pick, Betsy?"

"Sapphire blue."

"Great! I love that sapphire blue, too! I think your husband is going to be absolutely thrilled, Betsy," Fanny said. "And if he's not, let's throw the book at him, hahahaha!"

"Wrap up the call," the producer said in Fanny's earpiece.

"But seriously, I just know you and your husband are both going to enjoy and cherish this beautiful aquarium for years to come. Please let us know how much you love the tank when you get it, okay, Betsy? And thank-you for shopping with us at GHN!"

"I surely will," Betsy said. "Thanks, Fanny."

"Bye-bye, Betsy!" Fanny waved at the camera, her long fingernails taking several bows.

"Pick up the big snail, and show it off," instructed the voice in Fanny's earpiece.

"You know what I think might be fun?" Fanny said. "What do you say we get personal with some of these little fellas? This handsome guy, for instance."

Fanny used her hand to scoop up a large snail with an exquisitely colored shell, and presented it to the audience.

"Oopsy-daisy, snail overboard!" she said, fumbling for a moment, and accidentally dropping the creature back into the water.

"That little guy's a bit slippery, and I'm not too sure he likes being petted! Seems like he'd rather play with his friends in this incredibly realistic-looking cave right here," she said, recovering from the momentary glitch.

***

The sound of splashing water registered, and Edwina glanced up from her desk. A heavily made-up GHN presenter, dressed garishly in a sparkly gown that looked vaguely like a mermaid costume, appeared to have dropped something into an aquarium tank.

Edwina turned back to her work.

***

"Now, this fabulous cave is made out of a highly durable polyresin, and then it's painstakingly painted to give it this realistic look," Fanny said. "Doesn't it look exactly like real rock? This little cave, and these other items you see in the tank—like this adorable castle—are all available online at GHN. Just type in 'aquarium extras'."

"Take another call," said the voice in her earpiece.

"Perfect time to take another call," Fanny said.

"Hi, Carolyn! What do you think of this fabulous aquarium?"

"I love it, Fanny," Carolyn replied. "I think it's really beautiful, and I'm getting it for my kids for Christmas. Not sure where I'm going to hide it, yet, but I'm sure I'll think of something."

"That's great, Carolyn!" Fanny said. "And you can select whatever delivery date you want, so you can receive the aquarium as close to the holidays as you like. And thanks for reminding me about the holidays, because also available from GHN are these wonderful, decorative holiday background panels that slide in easily and clip onto the back of the tank. Let me show you how simple it is."

"These gorgeous photographic backgrounds simply slide in like this, and then clip onto the back of the tank, the same way you would with the colored panels that come with the aquarium. Easy as pie." Fanny demonstrated, fumbling with the clips.

"This amazing holiday panel shows a beautifully decorated Christmas tree next to a little fireplace with adorable fish shaped stockings hanging up. Look at those cute holly sprigs on the mantle! See how the fish are swimming in front this cozy scene? Isn't that priceless? It looks like your fish are celebrating Christmas in their own little home! Your kids will love it!"

"And for our Jewish viewers, check out this beautiful Hanukkah background scene. You've got your little lighted menorah, your dreidels, and chocolate coins, your plate of latkes, nice and hot, sitting on the table—the whole schmear! Did I say that word right, hahahaha?"

"Wow, that's great, Fanny," Carolyn-the-caller said. "I think I'll get that Christmas background for sure."

"Huge spike," said the voice in Fanny's earpiece. "Stay on the holiday stuff."

"Carolyn," Fanny said without missing a beat, "I am so thrilled you're getting this beautiful saltwater tank and Christmas background! It's so adorable, and the minute you install it, you'll never want to celebrate the holidays without it. Let me hand you over to our GHN operator, and she'll take care of you. Thanks so much for shopping with us. I hope your kids absolutely love their new tank, and their new fish family! Please make sure to take a picture on Christmas morning, and send it to us. I'll post it on my GHN page!"

"Okay, Fanny, I sure will," Carolyn replied.

"Bye-bye, now, Carolyn! Enjoy!"

"These are going quickly, friends! Let me run through the other holiday backgrounds we have for you to decorate your new fish tank," she said. "I think you're going to want to collect them all, once you see the high resolution photography on these background pictures, and all the incredible detail."

"We've got this Halloween scene with little fish dressed up like witches and goblins, which will probably be your kids' favorite! How cute are these little starfish-shaped candies, and jack-o-lanterns? Then we've got this Thanksgiving one for you, with this beautiful holiday feast and all the trimmings, set on an old-fashioned farm table, with a pumpkin centerpiece. See all the little fish dressed up in Pilgrim costumes? And look how cute this Valentine's Day one is, with these darling fish-shaped chocolate boxes and little seahorse cupids! It takes two seconds to switch these out, and the ones you're not using store easily at the back of the tank. Let me show you how easy they are to slide in and out."

"Whoops!" she exclaimed as the laminated panels slipped from her hands, and scattered on the floor. "Guess it's my day to be a butterfingers!"

"Well, never mind about that, because it looks like our aquarium has completely sold out! Thanks to all of you who purchased it, and congratulations on your beautiful new saltwater tank! I am so thrilled you're getting it."

"Please keep watching, because my good friend, Janie Schramm, is up next with the most amazing battery-operated, designer candles. You won't believe how realistic they look, and there's no messy wax to drip onto your beautiful table, and none of the danger of real candles! Then, I'll be back at four o'clock with Dr. Darlene and her iconic line of skin care. Let's face it ladies; who doesn't want to look twenty years younger––without surgery—hahahaha? Our Dr. Darlene is simply a *genius*! We call her 'the fountain of youth' around here. Don't forget to stay tuned all day long for more incredible deals!"

Her presentation had exceeded expectations, and Fanny was elated by selling out the aquariums. Her triumphant walk back to her dressing room was marred only slightly by the fact that her breakfast, which she had eaten too quickly, was not sitting well in her stomach. She probably just needed to lie down for a few minutes. She closed the dressing room door, kicked her shoes off across the room, and collapsed onto the sofa, flush with success.

Chapter 8

The jealous are troublesome to others, but a torment to
themselves.
~ William Penn

Will buzzed the gate at the entrance to GHN
Corporate Park, and flashed his badge to the security
man who appeared at the window of the little
guardhouse. Low, manicured hedges bordered the long
drive, and sweeping lawns were dotted with modern
sculptures on either side. Beyond the second security
gate, a complex of low-lying buildings came into view.
Will displayed his identification again, this time to a
camera, and spoke his name into an intercom. Just
ahead he could see the flashing lights of emergency
vehicles crowded around an entrance to one of the
buildings. He made his way through the cluster of
reporters and crime bloggers who had all managed, one
way or another, to talk their ways onto the scene.

The interior of the television studio building was
cavernous, and the enormity of it dwarfed everything
and everybody in it. Banks of cameras and television
lights were positioned toward fifteen different stages,
each set up in its own, individual, style of décor, and
layout.

Fanny's lifeless body had not been moved from the
sofa in her dressing room where she was found. Will
greeted Toby Czarlinski, the Medical Examiner, and
knelt on the floor beside him. Apart from the bluish
discoloration of Fanny's lips, and the general pallor one

would expect to see on a corpse, nothing stood out as an obvious cause of death. The ME lifted Fanny's hair off her neck, and gently felt her scalp near the base of the skull. He worked his way around her neck with his gloved hands, pressing lightly into her flesh.

"What've we got?" Will said.

"Dunno, yet. Possible heart attack," Toby replied. "Maybe a stroke. I'll know more when I get her into the office for examination. She had just come off the air, did you know?"

"Who found her?" Will asked.

"One of the other hosts, I think," Toby replied.

***

"Thank-you for agreeing to speak with me," Will said. "I know this must be difficult for you. I understand you're the one who found Miss Spendlove's body, is that right?"

"Yes, that's right."

Will observed Mary Lou Flowers across the table from where he sat in the deadened quiet of the empty conference room, where any sounds coming from the outside were muffled by the acoustics within. She was a woman of a certain age who dressed too youthfully, perhaps hoping it would distract from the toll that time and gravity had taken on her appearance. The stark distinction between a ropey, sagging neck, and the smooth, tautly stretched skin across her face, shouted 'face-lift'. The furrowed skin on her décolletage looked like the road map of an ancient city. Smoke and mirrors and redirection could only do so much. Mary Lou Flowers bore the strained look of someone who was about to burst at the seams.

Mary Lou's downcast eyes emphasized her false eyelashes, heavily applied with glue. In her lap she twisted a blue tissue through her fingers. Her nails were long and pointy, and Will wondered how she could manage to perform everyday tasks with such talons. He saw no sign that she had been crying. Her heavy make-up was undisturbed.

"Do you feel able to answer some questions?" he asked.

Mary Lou nodded.

"Did Miss Spendlove have any family—a husband, or a partner, or children?"

"No."

"What was your relationship with her like?" Will said.

"We'd been friends and colleagues since she first came to GHN," Mary Lou replied.

"When was that?" Will asked.

"Four years ago."

"How long have you been at GHN?" Will asked.

"Since the beginning," Mary Lou replied. "I was actually the original GHN girl, you know."

Will smiled.

"Did Fanny have any health issue that you were aware of?"

"No, as far as I know, her health was fine," Mary Lou said. "That's why this is all so shocking."

"Did she take drugs that you know of? Or, drink excessively?"

"Oh, no," Mary Lou answered. "I don't believe she took drugs, not that I was aware of, anyways. As for drinking—well, Fanny enjoyed her cocktails like most people."

Enjoyed her cocktails? Was Mary Lou trying to let Will know that Fanny had a drinking problem, without wanting to come out and say it?

"Were you and Fanny close friends?" he said.

"I'd say so. She was pretty green when she got here, so I took her under my wing," Mary Lou said. "She was a sweet kid, and very eager. I tried to help her out the best I could—showed her the ropes, stuff like that. This was her first, on-air job, you know."

"Oh? Is it usual for GHN to hire someone with no previous television experience?" Will asked.

"I kind of wondered about that, too," Mary Lou replied. "But I guess Fanny won them over. She could be very persuasive when she wanted to be. I heard she was pretty successful on Wall Street before she came here. She was a natural, born saleswoman, that's for sure. Besides, everybody gets six months of training at GHN before they go on the air, solo."

"Who did you hear that from?" Will said.

"Hear what?"

"That Fanny was successful on Wall Street."

"Oh, that," Mary Lou said, shifting in her chair. "Hm. I'm sorry, Detective; I can't honestly remember who told me that. It's just more or less common knowledge around here."

"Was that something you admired about her, Miss Flowers? Fanny's talent for winning people over?"

"Admired? I never really thought about it, I guess. Sometimes Fanny could be a little *too* forceful," she laughed uncomfortably. "She really thrived on competition, you know? I don't mean to gossip—any of the girls around her will tell you the same thing. Fanny was a real go-getter. She had lots of plans."

"Plans?'

"Well, you know," Mary Lou said, "I think she might've had ideas about starting her own jewelry and clothing line at the network, or something like that."

"Was that likely to happen?" Will said.

"It was a possibility. Like I said, Fanny was very persuasive," Mary Lou said.

"Do you know anything about her birth family?"

"Fanny never mentioned them, except to say she wasn't in touch with any of them," Mary Lou replied. "I wondered why, but she never said, and I didn't think it was right to ask. No, as far as I know, her health was fine," Mary Lou replied. "That's why this is all so shocking."

"Would you mind walking me through what happened—how you happened to discover the body?"

"Of course," she replied, weaving the tissue through her fingers. "I watched Fanny's show on a monitor, and there was something I wanted to talk to her about, so when the show wrapped, I went to her dressing room."

Mary Lou paused, and looked at Will. He nodded for her to continue.

"But when I knocked, there was no answer," Mary Lou said. "So I knocked again. Then, when there was still no answer, I opened the door a little bit, and peeked in."

"What were you expecting to see?" Will asked.

"What do you mean?" Mary Lou said.

"When you opened the door to the dressing room, what did you imagine you would see?" Will repeated.

Mary Lou was beginning to show some fluster.

"I don't know," she said. "Nothing in particular, I guess. Just Fanny changing clothes or whatever, like she usually did after a show."

"What was it you wanted to talk to her about?" Will said.

"I knew she'd been having a hard time lately with her boyfriend. I was worried about her, and wanted to see if she was okay."

Will sat tight without making any response. Silence had a way of encouraging some people to keep talking, and it was obvious there was much more to the story.

"The man Fanny had been seeing for a while recently broke off their relationship, and I knew she was unhappy about it," Mary Lou said. "She really wasn't very lucky in love, poor thing. I got the feeling she was hoping he might be 'the one'—you know, 'Mr. Right'. But then he dumped her," Mary Lou said. "I don't think she was expecting that."

"Do you think she could have been suicidal?"

"Suicidal?" Mary Lou replied. "Gosh, that never occurred to me. I guess it's possible."

"Do you have a name?" Will asked. "Of the boyfriend?"

Mary Lou paused to give her tissue a few more twists.

"Bobby McCloud," she replied.

"The actor?"

Chapter 9

Vanity is the quicksand of reason.
~ George Sand

Dust particles floated and swirled in a shaft of sunlight. An overhead fan whirred gently on low speed, and the occasional murmur of traffic drifted in from Main Street. Chief Val Burnstein sat with an unopened folder in front of her on the desk, and sipped coffee from an 'I Heart Grandma' mug. Taped up on the wall behind her was a grouping of children's drawings. Will sat across the desk.

"How was it up there?" the Chief asked.

"Usual stuff. A few eager beavers from the Mayor's Office were hanging around, trying to get information. The local news and radio guys rooting around for sound bites."

"What've we got?" she asked.

"White female, aged forty, name of Fanny Spendlove," Will said. "She's been a host at the GHN Network for the last four years. She was found in her dressing room, collapsed on a sofa, shortly after coming off the air."

"Nothing jumps out right away as cause of death," Will continued. "Toby thinks we might be looking at natural causes."

"But you think otherwise?" the Chief said, interpreting Will's expression.

"Too soon to call, I'd say," Will said. "I sure picked up some mixed signals when I interviewed the woman who found the body—Mary Lou Flowers, one of the other hosts, and a friend of the deceased. She didn't seem remotely moved by the fact that her colleague had just dropped dead."

"What else?" asked the Chief.

"Well, there's the fact that forty is a little young to keel over from natural causes," he said.

"C'mon, Will, you know as well as I do how common sudden deaths of apparently healthy, young individuals can be. We've seen people in their forties pop off before," she said.

"I know," he replied.

"Is there something else that's got you doubting natural causes?" she asked.

"Nothing in particular, just my gut," he said.

"Uh-huh," the Chief replied, tapping the eraser end of a pencil on the desk.

"Look," she said. "As long as we've got a death of undetermined origin on our hands, we may not know if we've got a 'whodunnit' or a 'did-anybody-do-it?' for a while. So, 'til we hear from Toby one way or the other, go ahead and ask around. Get her home address, and get a couple of uniforms to do cold knock-and-talks in her neighborhood. Interview the folks at GHN."

"Thanks," Will replied, rising to leave. "By the way, are you a Bobby McCloud fan?"

"Not particularly," she replied. "Why?"

"He was the deceased's ex-boyfriend."

Chapter 10

Pride that dines on vanity sups on contempt.
~ Ben Franklin

The door marked 'Hair & Makeup' was ajar. Will tapped on it.

"Miss Rubenstein?" he said.

A spritely, 70-ish woman with a gray, pixie haircut looked up from the sink where she was washing out makeup brushes. She eyed the GHN visitor's badge hanging from Will's neck.

"Yes?"

"Detective Tenney from the New Guilford Police. Okay if I ask you a few questions?"

"Sure," she replied. "Take a seat. I'll be with you in a second."

Will took a look around. Mirrored walls amplified the lighting. Shelves, open cupboards, rolling carts, and countertops spilled over with cosmetic products, tools, and paraphernalia. The business of vanity looked complicated.

Esther Rubenstein dried her hands, sat down in the styling chair next to Will, and swiveled to face him.

"What can I do for you, Detective?" she asked.

"I'd like to ask you a few questions about Fanny Spendlove. All right with you?"

"Fire away," she replied.

"Did you do makeup for all those actresses?" he asked, nodding toward the photographs on the wall.

"Every one of them," Esther said. "That's me on the end. I started out as a stage actress, you know. Light years ago. Those were some fun days in the theater, I'll tell you. Met some great people. Glamour and celebrity had a more restricted access back in the day. Stars were the real deal then, not like now, when anybody and everybody gets face time. It's all different nowadays."

Will nodded.

"How long have you been working here?" he asked.

"Believe it or not," Esther said, "I started here twenty-six years ago when the good folks at GHN opened their doors for business. An awful lot of people have come and gone since then, but not me. I'm the old lady of the operation."

"So, you must have started around the same time as Mary Lou Flowers?"

"That's right," Esther said.

"And, you've known Fanny Spendlove from the time she started here, is that right?" Will asked.

"Yes."

"Did you do her makeup on the day she died?"

"Yes, I did—every single layer of it. And her hair," Esther said.

"You don't seem particularly upset by her death," Will said.

"What's the point pretending?" Esther replied. "I didn't care for her very much."

"Why was that?"

"Because she treated me like the help," Esther said.

"Was there much conversation between the two of you that last day?" Will asked.

"Not really. Some of the girls like to chat when they're in the chair, but not everybody. It all depends," she said. "Some like to read, or even nap. A few of the girls will chat the whole time they're getting their hair and makeup done. I go with the flow. Whatever they want to do is fine by me."

"What about Fanny?"

"Like I said, I wasn't important enough for her," she said bluntly. "I'm only hair and makeup—the help, as it were. You have to understand something, Detective; basically, Fanny saw other people as supporting characters in a play starring herself. Other people existed mainly to serve her needs. So, no; Fanny did not open up to me in the chair, nor I to her. My only purpose as far as she was concerned was to make her look more attractive for the camera than she was in real life. Which, by the by, wasn't easy."

"How did she seem that day—the day she died?" Will asked. "Was she worried or upset about anything or anybody in particular? Did she seem ill?"

"Hardly," Esther replied, "except for being hung over, which was nothing new, it was business as usual. She studied her notes, used her phone, asked me to get her some breakfast from the cafeteria, which I did."

"Was that something she did often, ask you to bring her food?"

"Once in a while."

Will regarded Esther's body language. Her legs were crossed at the knee, her mouth set in a straight line, arms folded across her chest. Will sensed she was trying to decide how much to tell him. She was in a one-woman huddle, running plays in her head.

"What else can you tell me about Fanny?" he said.

"Let me put it this way," she said. "Fanny was not what she seemed to be. What you saw was not what you got. She was the biggest prima donna I've ever worked with—and that includes all the wonderful ladies I used to make up on Broadway, by the way, so you can imagine."

"'Wasn't what she seemed'," Will repeated. "How so?"

"She affected an entirely different personality on the air from who she really was. Let's just say she was unusually vain," Esther said. "She was obsessed with her appearance, and she went in for every kind of cosmetic procedure available. You name it—chemical peels; microdermabrasion; laser resurfacing; implants; plastic surgery, of course. Vain and narcissistic—that was Fanny."

"I would imagine cosmetic surgery is common in this line of work, though?" Will said. "Being concerned with your looks must be something of an occupational hazard for women who are under a lot of pressure to look good on TV?"

"To a point," Esther replied, "but Fanny went in for more procedures than most of the girls around here. Like I said, she was obsessed with how she looked."

"Anyway," Esther said, "why all the questions? I thought she died from natural causes?"

"We're just being thorough," Will said.

"Can you tell me anything about her relationship with Mary Lou Flowers?"

"I'd say those two were a case of 'keep your friends close, and your enemies closer'," she said. "Especially when Mary Lou took up with Brad Pilfer."

"Brad Pilfer?" Will asked.

"He's a big mucky muck around here, or thinks he is, anyway. Vice-President of something-or-other. Married, too. His little dalliance with Mary Lou was supposed to be a secret, but not much gets past me."

"How did Fanny find out?" Will asked.

"What can I say?" Esther said with a wry smile. "I just couldn't help myself. I must've been feeling bored that day. I knew Fanny had it in for Pilfer—she really hated the guy—so I figured it'd really get under her skin if she knew her so-called friend, Mary Lou, and he were enjoying some good, old-fashioned rumpy-pumpy behind the scenes. So, when I had Fanny in the chair one day, I let it casually slip out."

"How did she react?" he asked.

"I was surprised, but she ate it up—got very excited," Esther replied. "Wanted to hear all the details."

"You seem to know quite a bit about the goings-on around here," Will remarked.

"Scratch the surface of any workplace," Esther said, "and you'll find a full-blown soap opera. We're all grist for the gossip mill around here."

"What might people be saying about you?" Will asked.

"Me?" she snorted. "My claim to fame around here is my short-lived affair with Milton Babcock, I suppose."

"The cameraman?" he asked.

"That's the one," she said, eyeing Will carnivorously. "Sorry if I've shocked you, Detective. Women do have their needs, you know, even an old bag like me. Milton's a good-looking guy who happens to have a thing for older women, so can you blame me?"

"How long did the relationship last?"

"Just a few months; that's all," Esther replied. "It started to get awkward at work."

"Who broke it off?"

"It was mutual," Esther said. "We're on perfectly friendly terms these days, in case you were wondering."

"Can you tell me anything about Fanny's romantic life?" Will asked.

"I might," Esther replied. "Depends on what you mean by—"

"Miss Rubenstein," Will interrupted. Would you prefer to have this conversation at the police station?

I'd be happy to oblige. It's against the law to obstruct a police investigation. Did you know that?"

Esther glared icily at him.

"I suppose you know all about Fanny's former boyfriend?" she said.

Will did not respond.

"I suggest you speak to my ex-husband," she said.

"Why would I want to do that?" Will said.

"Because my ex happens to be Harry Crassman. Of the Crassman Talent Agency. He handles Fanny's ex-boyfriend. In fact, he pretty much has his hand up Bobby McCloud's backside. Harry calls all the shots. He's a regular wealth of information."

"Thank-you for your time, Miss Rubenstein," Will said, rising to leave.

"Oh, and good luck," she said. "Harry can be a real bastard."

Chapter 11

Curiosity will conquer fear even more than bravery will.
~ James Stephens

There was an airless, terrifying silence all around her as Edwina hurtled through the darkness, a heavy, metal license plate that said, 'information governance' hanging from a cumbersome chain around her neck. She tugged and pulled at it, but it would not budge. A series of sinister-looking optical distortions—ominous shafts of light bent and twisted by gravitational pull—told the unavoidable story of an event horizon looming just ahead. The enormous black hole within was swallowing up everything in sight, and Edwina was next. A taunting voice pierced through the darkness.

"Say hello to my little friend, the singularity!" it said, sounding uncannily like Al Pacino in *Scarface*.

Dammit! Where are the wormholes when you need one! Edwina thought, hoping she might somehow be able to circumvent the black hole at the last second. Her body tensed up in anticipation of the approaching impact, and she squeezed her eyes tightly shut.

Her heart was pounding against her chest when she suddenly awoke.

"Bad dream," she whispered hoarsely, as Will stirred from sleep.

He wrapped his arms around her, and fell back to sleep moments later. Edwina took a few deep breaths, closed her eyes, and tried to go back to sleep, too, but the gray light of dawn was creeping through the windows, and she knew she had got all the sleep she was going to get. Gently extricating herself from Will, she padded downstairs to the kitchen.

She filled the kettle, set it atop the wood stove, and added logs to the fire. Wrapping a wool shawl around her, she settled into the rocking chair by the window.

Pale shafts of early morning light filtered through the branches of the trees, glinting. Birds began to chirp and sing, and commenced pecking sunflower seeds from the feeder hanging in the sugar maple. These particulars of daybreak eluded Edwina that morning, however, because her focus did not extend beyond the window panes, where a string of mathematical sequences was written out across the glass. As she scrutinized the expressions, and performed a few calculations in her head, a geyser of steam issued silently from the kettle, unnoticed. Her focus was wholly absorbed by a particularly problematic partial differential equation. She had fallen under its spell.

Even Will's presence in the kitchen sometime later did not interrupt her reverie. He hoped he would not startle her by calling her name softly several times. When she finally looked up, she regarded his unshaven face and tousled hair with abundant tenderness, and wanted nothing more than for them to return to bed. But, time did not allow; she had a train to catch, he reminded her. It was the weekend of the MIT conference, where she was scheduled to speak the following day. There was no negotiating for a later time slot; her session had already been announced and advertised in the schedule. And besides, she had promised to meet her old colleague, Phillip Kimby, for lunch after her talk. There was no time for dilly-dallying this morning.

***

Edwina was pleasantly surprised to discover that the hotel where the conference committee had booked her was a charming jewel of a place off the beaten path, housed in an historic, brick building, walking distance from MIT. Outside her window, the Charles River was dotted with an array of sailboats, yachts, houseboats, sight-seeing boats, kayaks, and so on. She sat by the window, and watched as their skippers navigated their ways to who-knows-where.

After unpacking, she took a bath in a gleaming tub surrounded by gray marble, and settled in for the night. Sprawled on the king-sized bed, wrapped in a plush robe with the hotel insignia on the chest pocket, she ordered room service, and watched Hitchcock's 1966 *Torn Curtain*. She and Will messaged back and forth throughout the evening.

***

The auditorium was filled to standing room capacity when Edwina arrived the following morning, full of nervous butterflies. It was the anticipation and the waiting that gave her the flutters, but the moment she spoke her first words, and filled the dead air, she felt relaxed and at ease. The subject matter of quantum entanglement carried her aloft for two hours, just as playing a beautiful piece of music would a musician.

Her talk was well received—some would later say it was the highlight of the conference. The Q and A session that followed had to be cut short by the moderator in order to accommodate the next speaker's scheduled time slot. At the end, when a group of audience members followed Edwina out of the auditorium, she was happy to chat with them for as long as she could, checking her watch to make sure she wouldn't be late for her lunch date. When she did eventually have to excuse herself from the group, she handed out cards with her contact information, in case anyone wanted to carry on the conversation online.

Halfway through the short walk to the restaurant, she realized she was ravenously hungry, and quickened her pace to meet Phillip Kimby. She wondered what sort of restaurant he had chosen, and if he would look any different.

Edwina found the formal interior of *La Gavroche* somewhat intimidating. She gazed around at the starched, pale pink table linens, adorned with fresh flowers cascading from silver epergnes. Industrial-sized planters were potted with weeping fig trees that reached upwards toward an elaborate, coffered ceiling. Lush scenes of Versailles were hand-painted on the silk-covered walls, and subtly illuminated by hidden lighting fixtures. Waiters stood discreetly at the ready in shadowy recesses. Altogether, the place had an overly dramatic affect.

George, the diminutive Maître' d, pursed his lips at the sight of Edwina's ensemble of a blazer and jeans, and stoically escorted her to the corner table where Phillip Kimby was waiting. Phillip rose to greet her.

"Nice place, Phil," she smiled. "Long way from our Student Union days."

"Good to see you," Phillip said warmly. A blue, silk tie was tucked nattily into the tweed vest he wore under a bespoke jacket, creating a general impression that was pure Saville Row. Apart from this upgrade in wardrobe, he looked much the same as when Edwina had last seen him, some years earlier.

"How are you? You look fantastic!" he said.

"Thanks, Phil. I'm doing well." Edwina said. "You?"

"Terrific!" he said, pulling out her chair. "Thanks for making the time for lunch. I've been looking forward to catching up. By the way, you were brilliant this morning, but then again, I expected that."

"Oh?" Edwina replied. "I didn't know you were there."

"Of course," Phillip said, "I wouldn't have missed it. I've been following your work for years, and I was eager to hear your talk, and not just because what you're doing fits in rather wonderfully with what we're trying to do down in Maryland. But I promise I won't bug you about your decision, and try to change your mind."

A waiter appeared, delicately cradling a bottle of wine as if it were a baby, and poured some out for Phillip to taste, who signaled his approval with a nod.

"What do you think?" Phillip asked after Edwina had tried it.

"Delicious," she replied.

***

"So, how is dear old Cushing these days?" Phillip said over a first course of *Tartare de Bar a' L'Avocat et Citron Vert*. "New Guilford is coming up in the world––or down, depending how you look at it—didn't I read something about a murder?"

"A murder?" Edwina replied. "Oh, you mean that poor woman who died at the home shopping network? I don't think it was a murder, although it's still being investigated, so I suppose it might be."

"Well, it sounded mysterious, the way she died so suddenly, with no apparent cause. Must be exciting having inside information," Phillip said.

Edwina looked at him quizzically

"Sorry," he chuckled. "Background is part of my job at the Agency. I guess it's become a habit. Nothing overly invasive, I assure you. So, yes, I know about your relationship with William Tenney. Must be fun dating a police detective, and being privy to inside scoop. Enlighten me about the investigation."

Phillip's comments rankled slightly, and made Edwina feel defensive. Phillip's Big Brother routine annoyed her, and she tried to brush it aside.

"All I really know is that the dead woman—Fanny Spendlove—was a host on the home shopping channel," Edwina replied, "and that she had just come off the air when she collapsed and died. They think food poisoning might be a possibility, or a heart attack."

"That doesn't sound nearly as exciting as murder. Know anything else about her?"

Edwina shook her head.

"Not really, no."

"So, no suspects, yet?" Phillip asked.

"Suspects?" she replied. "They don't even know what caused her death. Let alone, if anybody did it. Why so curious?"

"No special reason," Phil said. "Occupational hazard, I guess."

The rest of the meal was relaxing and convivial. Edwina's unease at the formality of La Gavroche was vanquished by the wine, the food, and conversation. They swapped stories and gossip, and rehashed memories from their student days. The subject of Edwina becoming part of 'the team in Maryland' did not come up until the end of the meal, after coffee and dessert.

"I'll have a brandy, please, Michel," Phillip said to the waiter. "Edwina?"

"Not for me, thanks," she replied.

Phillip waited for the brandy to arrive before reaching into his jacket pocket, and producing a packet. He laid it down on the table, and pushed it across to Edwina.

"I hope you can forgive an old friend one, final push?" he said. "Are you absolutely positive you don't want to join us at The Agency? It's pretty exciting work, you know. We could use your brain, Edwina."

She stared at the envelope, naturally curious. She thought about what Paolo had said about the inevitability of the next generation of cyber cryptology, and mightn't she like to be part of its arrival?

"Thanks, Phil. I appreciate the offer. I really do. But I'm happy with things the way they are. My work at Cushing is excitement enough."

Chapter 12

Vanity working on a weak mind produces every sort of mischief. . . .
~ Jane Austen

"Morning, doc," the Chief said.

Stainless steel work surfaces gleamed under the harsh lights of the examining room. Yellowed anatomical charts in black frames hung on the walls, but otherwise the place was spotless, and up to date. Will and the Chief removed surgical gloves from the dispenser on the wall, and pulled them on for the viewing.

Fanny Spendlove's body lay on a table, covered by an evidence sheet from her toes to her clavicle. Chief Burnstein and Will hovered over the examination table, awaiting information about the cause and manner of her death. The Chief glanced at her watch with impatience as the ME took his time tidying up at the corner sink. She never got used to the fact that Toby would not be rushed or cajoled. Whatever the doc had to say would all come out in good time. In *his* time. Toby Czarlinski had run the Medical Examiner's Office for twenty years with exemplary efficiency, always at his own, resolute pace.

"Found a few things of interest," he said at last, approaching the table.

"What looked at first like a stroke, pretty quickish turned into something else," Toby said. "Something a little more complicated. Fanny Spendlove died from respiratory arrest—cessation of breathing due to a complete paralysis of the diaphragm and chest muscles."

"What caused it?" the Chief said.

"Most likely it was the result of a reaction to a toxin," Toby replied.

"What kind of toxin?" asked the Chief.

"Dunno, yet. We'll have to wait for the tox report, which I sent out last night."

"I went through her stomach contents," he continued, "on the assumption that the toxin in question was introduced into her system through food or drink, but no dice. It wasn't food poisoning."

"What about an allergic reaction of some kind?" Will said.

"Looks like it," replied Toby. "Looky here."

The ME gently removed Fanny's left arm from under the sheet. Picking up her hand and holding it in his, he rotated her palm upwards. Then he handed Val a magnifying glass.

"I thought maybe drugs, so I did a thorough check of her entire body and head for injection sites. Turns out there is one, lone point of entry where a toxin might have entered her bloodstream, and I found it right here," the doc said. "Took me a while. I removed her false fingernails, and looked underneath her real nails. Then I spotted it, right here, in the webbing between this index and middle finger. Look at these little petechiae formed into a tiny cluster of hemorrhages. And see the blanching and swelling there?"

Chief Burnstein spent some time examining Fanny's hand before she handed the magnifying glass to Will.

"So, some sort of poison—or allergen or whatever— was introduced into her system through this tiny pin prick?" Will said.

"Looks like it," replied Toby.

"So, when would the poison have been administered?" asked the Chief. "I mean, how long before it killed her?"

"Can't say 'til I know what kind of toxic compounds we're dealing with," Toby replied.

"Is is possible she administered it herself?" Will asked.

"A person could, but I'd say it's doubtful," Toby said. "Seems like a pretty screwy place to inject yourself. And, if it was suicide, why try to hide the point of entry?"

"What if it was suicide," Will said, "and she was trying to make it look like murder?"

"I doubt it," Toby said. "Suffocating like this would have been an extremely unpleasant death. There are easier, less traumatic ways to do away with yourself."

"So, what are you thinking for manner?" the Chief asked.

"I'd rule out suicide," replied Toby. "There's a chance it was accidental—she could have pricked herself on something sharp that had come into contact with the toxin. It's obvious she didn't die from natural causes, so we can rule that out, too. If it turns out that someone else administered the poison, then you'll be looking at a homicide. I'll be able to tell you a lot more once I know what kind of toxin we're dealing with."

"Anything you can do to hurry up the report?" the Chief said.

"See what I can do, Val," Toby replied. But for the moment, we have a few more points of interest up north."

Fanny's lifeless face looked forsaken and forlorn. There was not a hint or reminder of the glamour she presented on television. Without the aid of hair extensions, her natural hair was lank and scruffy. Scrubbed clean from any trace of makeup, she was rather homely. Toby held her jaw, and gently turned her head to one side, pulling her hair back from her face.

"Nothing too unusual about this," he said, pointing to tiny incision marks around Fanny's ears."

"Face lift?" said the Chief.

"Yup," replied Toby, "but look at this."

Will and Chief Burnstein leaned in closer, and saw a discreet, white scar—about an inch long—on Fanny's neck.

"Ever heard of chondrolaryngoplasty?" Toby asked.

"Come again?" the Chief said.

"TCR? Thyroid cartilage reduction?" Toby said helpfully. "How about 'tracheal shave'? No?"

"We talking about Adam's apple reduction?" Will said.

"And we have a winner," Toby said. "She had her Adam's apple shaved down at some point in her adulthood, so it wouldn't stick out so much, and this little scar is the memento from the procedure."

"Which brings me to this," he said, slowly pulling the sheet away from the lower region of her body.

"You're going to need to get just a little bit closer in order to see this properly," he continued.

"As you can see," he said, gently shifting the skin around Fanny's genital area to one side to reveal more scarring, "Miss Spendlove did not arrive on the planet as a female. Not in this lifetime, anyway."

***

"Seems surprising that GHN would hire a transgender host," Val said on the drive back to the police station. "Think they knew about it?"

"I seriously doubt it," Will said. "I'd imagine it was something Fanny kept to herself."

"The first order of business is for you to go back to GHN. See if you can find out if anybody knew her secret. It could help us with motive."

"Huh," Will said. "I was just thinking, now my interview with the make-up woman—Esther Rubenstein—makes more sense to me. She was very evasive with some of her answers, and I wonder if it's because she knew about Fanny being transgender. A makeup person would have plenty of opportunity to see that scar on Fanny's neck—or signs of hair loss pattern, or skin texture—stuff like that."

"Why not tell you during the interview?" Val said. "Why avoid mentioning it?"

"Beats me," Will replied. "Maybe she wanted to have the upper hand with me. Maybe she was blackmailing Fanny, threatening to let GHN know the truth about her. I wouldn't put it past her. She was very upfront about not liking Fanny."

"Any luck reaching Fanny's parents?"

"Yeah," Will replied. "I finally got the father on the phone. He barely reacted when I told him Fanny had died. I said we would keep him up to date with the investigation. He was very polite, but he didn't say very much. Thanked me for calling. That was about it."

"Maybe now we know why," said Val. "Maybe they were estranged after Fanny had the surgery."

They pulled into the police station parking lot. Will dropped Val off, and headed to GHN.

***

He found Milton Babcock in the cafeteria, seated alone, reading the latest issue of *Digital Camera Magazine*.

"Mr. Babcock?" Will said, showing his identification. "Mind if I ask you a few questions?"

"Sure," Milton replied, laying down the magazine. "Please, sit down."

Will ran a quick eye over the piles of empty bowls and plates on the tray in front of the cameraman. Aside from his corpulent figure, Milton Babcock had striking blue eyes and a rather handsome face.

"I skipped breakfast," Milton said sheepishly.

"I understand you were operating the camera on the day Fanny Spendlove died. Is that right?" Will said.

"Yes, I was," Milton replied. "Am I in some sort of trouble?"

"No, no," Will replied. "Nothing like that. We're just gathering information about the day Fanny died. We're talking to everyone."

"I see," Milton said.

"Did you have a close relationship with Fanny?"

"Close?" Milton repeated. "I wouldn't exactly say, close; no. We just worked together, but we weren't friends."

"What was your general impression of her?"

"How do you mean?" the cameraman asked.

"Well," Will said, "did you like her?"

"She was all right," Milton said. "Not as friendly as some of the ladies. She was kind of stand-offish. I got the feeling she thought she was better than everybody else."

"Uh-huh. I wonder if you could walk me through exactly what happened that day?"

"Sure thing," Milton said. "It was pretty much business as usual. Fanny was selling an aquarium, which was a big deal, because GHN has never sold a saltwater aquarium before, and I understand a few of the hosts were hoping they'd get to present it. I guess it was kind of a status thing. Anyway, Fanny did great, and we sold out of them during her presentation. She was really good at her job; I'll say that for her."

"Uh-huh," Will nodded. "What happened then?"

"Nothing, really," Milton said. "Like I said, she sold a ton of aquariums, and after her segment finished, she went back to her dressing room."

"Did she say anything to you?" Will asked.

"Now that you mention it, she did ask me to get her a bottle of sparkling water when she walked off the set," Milton answered. "I guess she wasn't feeling too good. Now I wish I'd hung around to make sure she was okay; maybe I could have helped her."

"I don't think there's anything you could have done," Will said. "Did she seem upset about anything that day? Did you happen to see her arguing with anybody, or anything like that?"

"No, she didn't seem upset at all," Milton replied. "In fact, she seemed excited about the show. You know—because the aquarium thing was such a big deal."

"Right," Will said, making notes.

Milton scanned the contents of his tray, as if hoping an extra serving of chocolate pudding might appear from somewhere.

"Mr. Babcock, one last question for now," Will said. "Can you think of anything else—anything at all—that might've seemed different about that day? Anything out of the ordinary, anything unusual?"

"Nah, I don't think so," he replied. "Unless—I mean, it's probably nothing—but I remember seeing one of the execs hanging around the set, and I wondered what he was doing."

"Who was it?"

"Mr. Pilfer."

"Is it unusual to see him on the set?"

"Yes," Milton replied. "The executives' offices are in a different part of the building, and they don't generally visit the set. There's no real reason for them to be down here."

"Do you know why Mr. Pilfer was on the set that day?" Will asked.

"There was a tour group that morning, so I guess he was probably helping out with that," Milton replied. "Tour days are a real pain in the neck."

"Why is that?" Will inquired.

"They clutter up the studio with all those people wandering around. Plus, you never know if somebody's going to disappear somewhere," Milton replied. "I remember a few years ago, one of the presenters found a tour member snooping around her dressing room. People can be so nuts, you know?"

"So, I get that you and Fanny were not exactly friends," Will said. "I'm just wondering if you ever heard any, uh, gossip about her? Ever hear anything about her personal life?"

The cameraman looked at Will with a blank face.

"You mean, about her dating that actor?" Milton replied. "Believe me, Fanny made sure everybody knew about that."

"Anything else, though, besides that?" Will said. "I understand you and Esther Rubenstein were involved for a while. Did the two of you ever discuss Fanny? Maybe something about her past?"

Walter blushed at the mention of Esther.

"No, I don't think we ever did."

***

During the following hours spent interviewing crew members, staff, and hosts, not one of them mentioned, alluded to, or seemed to be hiding knowledge of the fact that Fanny was transgender. It appeared to have been a well kept secret. When he finished talking to hosts and crew members, Will headed up to the third floor, where the executive offices were.

He stepped off the elevator into a stylish foyer where life-sized posters of the GHN hosts were displayed on the walls. Posed in variously stilted ways, each had been photo-shopped in front of one exotic background or another—The Great Sphinx of Giza; Victoria Falls; the Taj Mahal; and so on. Fanny's picture was still hanging among them, and showed her outfitted grandly in traditional highland garb, posing against a virtual background of Edinburgh Castle.

He was met in a sleek reception area by Vice President in charge of marketing, Bradley Pilfer. A navy blue suit jacket hugged his mid-section, making him look vaguely sausage-like. The raspberry-colored silk handkerchief in his jacket pocket matched his tie, and a pair of silver cufflinks bore the GHN logo. His flushed complexion suggested either a recent workout, or a drinking habit, and Will figured on the latter.

"Take a pew, Detective," Mr. Pilfer said, leading Will into his office. "What can I do for you?"

"Thanks for meeting with me," Will said. "As you probably know, we're investigating the death of Fanny Spendlove. All right if I ask you a few questions?"

"Of course," he replied, shifting in his chair. "But I thought Fanny died from natural causes—what is the reason for the investigation?"

"At the present time, we're calling the cause of death 'undetermined origin'," Will said. "Meaning, a cause has not been officially determined, so we're looking into all possibilities, until we know for certain. It's standard procedure."

Brad Pilfer's complexion deepened to a darker hue.

"We're all devastated by this tragedy," he said. "Fanny was one of our brightest stars here at the network. Her death is a terrible loss to the GHN family. Just awful. She was a terrific gal, you know."

"Can you tell me who hired her?" Will asked.

"I did, as a matter of fact," Mr. Pilfer said, "but I'm not sure what relevance that could have on anything."

"Possibly none," Will said, "but I wanted to clear something up for myself."

"Oh?"

"It's just that I understand you and Fanny were not on particularly friendly terms," Will said. "Did something happen to cause a rift between you? Was there some sort of falling out?"

Of particular note during the interview was the fact that Mr. Pilfer was something of a human barometer. His skin tone appeared to change according to his level of discomfort. This last question caused the color to drain from his expression completely, leaving him looking ashen. He cleared his throat, and straightened his pocket handkerchief. The hamster in his brain was racing around that little wheel at full speed.

"First of all," he replied, "I wouldn't say Fanny and I were on bad terms. I can't imagine who might have told you that. We were on excellent terms. True, we didn't necessarily see eye to eye about everything—"

"Such as?" Will interjected.

"I beg your pardon?"

"You just said that you and Fanny didn't see eye to eye on everything. Like what, for instance?" Will repeated. "What did you not see eye to eye about?"

Will was amazed when people like Brad Pilfer tried to hide behind doublespeak and vagaries. They were language conmen, and took umbrage at being held to their words. They were people who blithely refashioned the meanings and usages of words as they went along, to suit their own purposes.

"Oh, I don't know," he chuckled. "Nothing, really—you know—little things, like which items should get promoted as feature of the day, how best to present them, price points—things like that."

"How did Fanny first come to your attention?" asked Will.

"That's actually a funny story," Mr. Pilfer said.

"Talk about a small world—Fanny and I knew each other before I came to GHN. We used to work at the same investment firm in New York—McAndrews Larsen."

"Uh-huh," Will said, marveling that VP Pilfer thought this scant amount of information was enough to suffice.

"What more can you tell me about that?" Will asked.

"I'm not sure there's much more to tell," replied Mr. Pilfer. "I worked in accounting. Fanny was an assistant to one of the senior investors. I decided on a change of course in my career, and took the job at GHN. Fanny eventually left McAndrews Larsen, too, and ended up in this neck of the woods. When she found out I worked at GHN, she got in touch with me, and I hired her."

"Were you and Fanny friends at McAndrews Larsen?" Will said.

"Not really, no," Mr. Pilfer said. "More like, acquaintances."

"That's quite a coincidence," Will said. "Two employees at the same investment firm in New York City ending up at GHN. And very generous of you to hire her on at GHN."

VP Pilfer shrugged it off with a smile.

"As they say, truth can be stranger than fiction, I guess," he said, his complexion deepening a shade.

"I understand Fanny had no prior television experience," Will said. "Is that unusual, for a GHN presenter to be hired without previous experience in front of a camera?"

"It happens from time to time," Mr. Pilfer said. "Fanny was a natural. Highly presentable, and a quick learner. She was a natural saleswoman. I had no doubt she would do well."

"Do you know why she left McAndrews Larsen?" Will said.

"No, I'm afraid I don't."

"Did you know anything at all about her personal life?" Will asked.

"No, not really. Like what?"

"Anything," Will said. "Anything at all. Whether she was married, or seeing anyone—her hobbies; outside interests—that sort of thing. The things people get to know about each other when they work together. And, you and Fanny worked together twice."

"Oh, I see what you mean," Mr. Pilfer said, trying to sound like a regular guy instead of an evasive stumblebum. "Sorry not to be of more help, Detective, but Fanny and I always kept our relationship on a professional level. I'm afraid I really don't know anything at all about her personal life."

"Just one last question, for the moment, sir. Did you happen to visit Fanny's aquarium set shortly before she went on the air?"

"No, I don't think so," Mr. Pilfer replied. "Oh, wait a second. Now that you mention it, yes," he continued. "We had a tour group in the studio that day. I was on hand to help out with that—you know, make sure things ran smoothly."

"Uh-huh," Will said. "About how long would you say you were in and around Fanny's aquarium set that day?"

"Oh, probably about half an hour."

"Okay," Will said, making a note.

"Is this your wife and children?" Will asked, pointing at a framed photo on the desk.

"Yes."

"Very handsome family," Will said.

"Thank-you."

"Actually, there was one other thing I wanted to ask you about, Mr. Pilfer. It's about your relationship with Mary Lou Flowers."

Brad Pilfer's coloring changed in an instant.

"What about it?" Mr. Pilfer said.

"It is sexual in nature; isn't that correct?" Will said.

"Oh, god, biggest mistake of my life," he gasped, scrabbling around in a desk drawer. "Will my wife have to be told about it?"

"Are you all right, sir?"

"High blood pressure," Mr. Pilfer said, swallowing a pill.

"Take a few breaths," Will said. "We can do this later, if you prefer."

"No, it's fine," said Mr. Pilfer, closing his eyes. "I'm okay. I just need a moment."

"I'm a weak man, Detective. Mary Lou offered herself to me, and I couldn't refuse. Simple as that. She's a very attractive woman, you know."

"Honestly," he continued. "I don't really know what I could have been thinking when I started up with her. She turned out to be very needy. She's an emotionally unstable alcoholic—an absolute train wreck. I don't know how much longer we're going to be able to keep her at the network. She's actually gone on the air once or twice after she's been drinking—can you believe it?"

Will was silent.

"I've been meaning to break it off for some time. As you see, I have a lovely wife, and two wonderful kids. I really don't know what I could have been thinking," he repeated, shaking his head. "It's just that Mary Lou is a very, uh, passionate individual."

"Why didn't you mention this relationship earlier?" Will asked.

"I'm sorry about that, Detective. I really am. That was stupid of me. I guess I was embarrassed. And I didn't think it had anything to do with Fanny's death. Now, wait a minute—you don't think it *does* have anything to do with Fanny's death—do you, Detective?" Mr. Pilfer said, changing color again.

***

Will sat across the desk from Chief Val in her office.

"Been on the phone with McAndrews Larsen," he said, "the investment firm in New York where Brad Pilfer and Fanny Spendlove worked before they both ended up at GHN."

"He's the one who hired her at GHN," Val said.

"Right. Turns out Pilfer got caught with his hand in the cookie jar back at McAndrews Larsen. Evidently there were some accounting discrepancies on his watch, and everything pointed to him. The company let him go, but they gave him the opportunity to pay back the funds, instead of pressing charges."

"Lucky Mr. Pilfer," said the Chief. "I imagine the investors wouldn't have been too happy if they knew the firm was being embezzled."

"Right," said Will. "So, Pilfer was able to leave the firm squeaky clean, because McAndrews Larsen didn't want to go on public record about the whole thing, and lose most their clients overnight. And, with no criminal record, Pilfer landed a good job at GHN."

"Then," the Chief added, "Fanny Spendlove shows up. Maybe she threatens to out his secret?"

"Unless he agrees to hire her on at GHN," Will said.

"It explains why Pilfer was no fan of hers," said the Chief. "Get a hold of Fanny's bank statements, would you?"

"Will do."

"Anything else?" she said.

"I was thinking about Mary Lou Flowers," Will said, "how she had kind of a chip on her shoulder about Fanny. It's possible she's involved in this thing with Pilfer."

"That's a thought," Val said.

"You know, the more time I spend at GHN, the more the place creeps me out," he said.

"What do you mean?" Val said.

"Aside from all the back-biting and bed-hopping, they all seem like a bunch of con men—they'll say anything if it'll sell stuff that nobody needs in the first place."

"Come on, Will," Val said. "That's what salespeople do."

"It's the phony personal touch that gets me," he said, "the way they play on people's emotions. The other day when I was up there watching a show go out live, I heard a host say something like, 'This vacuum cleaner is *life-altering*, ladies. It'll give you a whole, new sense of purpose in life. Please connect with me on my personal page here at GHN. Let's share our stories, blah, blah.'"

"Free country," Val shrugged.

"I suppose," Will said, "but what kind of person is willing to call a vacuum cleaner 'life-altering'? Do they even *know* they're bullshitting, or is it second nature? I mean, if you're going to play around with reality like that, just so you can make a sale, then pretty soon, words won't mean anything at all."

"Okay, Will," said the Chief. "You're getting a little philosophical on me, boy. How about getting those bank statements?"

***

Once Will had secured the information he needed from Fanny's bank, he headed back to GHN. He approached the set where a live segment was in progress, and found an unobtrusive place to stand in the shadows next to Milton Babcock, who was operating the camera.

"I'm telling you what!" Janie Schramm said. "These shoes are *literally* flying out the door! Please don't miss out on them. For only four installments of twenty bucks and change, you can get these babies home—but only until midnight tonight, when this special offer goes away. For*ever*! You know you can't go wrong with this iconic shoe brand."

"Now, listen, ladies," Janie Schramm said. "I know these are some crazy and challenging times we're living in. Heck, who can even follow all the wall-to-wall political jabber that's going on? It's nuts, right? I don't even pay attention to it, anymore."

"So, what do you say we focus on the things we *really* care about—the important stuff—like great shoes, hahahaha!"

"Green is dead," said the voice in Janie's earpiece.

"Now, I encourage you ladies—especially if you're shy about trying new colors—to pick up this fabulous mint green. I am so insanely in love with this shade! I own a pair! This color goes with just about everything in my closet. You're going to absolutely love them the second you get them home, I promise! Mint green is the new neutral, for heaven's sake! You need these shoes! I'm telling ya': You. Need. These. Shoes!"

"Is she wearing an earpiece?" Will whispered to Milton Babcock, who nodded without looking up from the camera.

When a customer was put through on the air, Janie did not stop talking long enough for the thwarted caller to get in a word, and the call was soon ended.

"Rein it in, Janie," said the voice in her earpiece.

"You guys, I *promise* I'll let the next caller do the talking!" Janie said apologetically. "They don't call me 'psycho shoe girl' for nothing, right, hahaha? I just get so darned excited about the amazing shoes and boots we offer here at GHN, I can't even control myself! It's crazy, right? My kids are always telling me they think I'm nuts—it's so cute!"

Janie Schramm's rapid fire delivery made Will wonder if GHN drug tested their employees, and he made a note of it. When he noticed Janie glancing at an index card partially secreted behind the display of shoes, he made another note. Had Fanny referred to written notes when she was on the air for the last time? Were the shows scripted to some degree? Had she been instructed to handle the snail? If there were notes from Fanny's last show he wanted to see them. They might have a tale to tell.

Chapter 13

Love is friendship that has caught fire.
~ Ann Landers

During the ride home from the train station, Edwina regaled Will with the events of her weekend in Boston, beginning with her standing-room-only talk, and culminating with a detailed recap of her posh lunch at *La Gavroche* with Phil Kimby.

"Now, you," she said as they pulled into the driveway of her cottage. "Fill me in on the investigation. Tell me everything that's been going on."

Will hopped out of the truck, and grabbed two bags of groceries from the back.

"Picked up some stuff for you at Dan's," he said, "but I can't stay. I have to work tonight. Can you meet me for lunch tomorrow? I'll catch you up on everything then."

***

Earl's Café was full at lunchtime more often than not, popular as it was with both town and gown, including a devoted cadre of regulars. Owner Earl Dufresne kept a corner table near the front reserved for this group of old-timers who came in every day. All retired, a few of them showed up each morning for breakfast, and stayed until the evening; others were in and out throughout the day. Some of them had known Earl since his days as a tugboat captain in Portsmouth.

"Hey, Will," the pretty, young woman working behind the counter said when he came in. She gave him a high-wattage smile, and held it. Edwina witnessed this from the back booth, where she had been waiting for Will. She assumed the twenty-something woman was a Cushing student with a part-time job.

"Who was that?" Edwina asked when Will sat down.

"Earl's niece," Will replied. "She's taking over the place from him when he retires."

Jealousy was sufficiently unfamiliar to Edwina that it took her a few moments to recognize it as such, but even so, the discomfort of it was soon trumped by curiosity about the investigation, and within a very short time, Edwina sat, rapt, having forgotten all about Earl's pretty niece, as Will quietly discussed the case.

"Fanny Spendlove?" Edwina said, washing down a mouthful of chicken pot pie with beer. "Which one is she?"

Will pulled up an image on his phone.

"Long, dark hair; sturdy figure," he said, showing Edwina.

"Oh sure, I've seen her," Edwina said. "What happened?"

"All we know is that she collapsed in her dressing room minutes after she came off the air," Will said. "She stopped breathing. Suffocated to death before anybody found her. Toby discovered a toxin in her system—he doesn't know what it is, yet—and a tiny pin prick between two of her fingers."

Edwina drizzled honey onto a piece of cornbread. "A pin prick?"

"That's how Toby thinks the toxin got into her system. We're waiting for the toxicology report," Will said.

"Could it be suicide?" Edwina said.

"According to Toby, her death would have been a gradual and nasty one, so suicide doesn't seem likely," Will said, "but we're not ruling it out, yet. Another possibility is that it was accidental, and that she somehow stuck herself with something that had come into contact with the toxin."

"That doesn't seem very likely," Edwina said.

"I agree, but we have to consider it," he replied. "Theoretically it's possible, I guess you could reach for something, and you don't notice a sharp object nearby, like a pin, or a bit of wire, or a nail. I've jabbed myself on sharpened pencils before."

"And what kind of deadly toxin would find its way to a pencil point?" Edwina said.

"Unlikely, I agree," Will said.

"So, are you stuck in neutral until you get the toxicology report?" Edwina said.

"No," Will said. "In fact, we have a strong line of inquiry to pursue. Fanny was transgender—born, Gus Prestopino. I don't think I've ever seen the color drain out of Val's face like it did when Toby pulled the sheet away, so we could get a good, close look at the telltale signs. I think it was the element of surprise that got her—neither of us was expecting it."

"Do you think GHN knew about it?" Edwina said.

"If they did, nobody's admitting to it," Will said.

"So, Fanny Spendlove was born Gus Prestopino, and she was passing herself off all this time at GHN, without anyone knowing?" Edwina said. "That wouldn't be very good for business, would it, if it came out?"

"What do you mean?" Will said.

"What if someone at GHN found out Fanny was transgender, and let it be known to her bosses?" Edwina said. "I'm just saying that the home shopping crowd is probably fairly conservative, and having a transgender host might not be considered especially good for business."

"So—what—the GHN mafia had her killed?" Will said. "An executive at the network put a hit out on her?"

"Okay—when you put it that way, it sounds ridiculous," Edwina said. "I'm just saying, if Fanny was keeping it a secret, and somebody outed her, the network probably wouldn't have been very happy about it.

"Another possibility is that maybe Fanny was using her secret for leverage—maybe threatening to out herself if she didn't get something she wanted—a big raise—or her own show—or something like that. Maybe she was trying to use the information to her advantage, and it backfired."

"Yeah," Will said, "but I can also imagine a scenario where GHN would *want* to promote a transgender host—use it to their financial advantage by connecting with a new sector of shoppers. And, besides, if they wanted to get rid of Fanny, why not just cancel her contract?"

"On what grounds—sexual discrimination? That would be illegal, and Fanny probably could have sued, and a high profile law suit like that would be even worse for business. What else do you know about her?" Edwina said.

"She used to work at an investment firm in New York," Will said. "There's an executive at GHN who worked there at the same time Fanny did. They knew each other. He was let go for embezzling from the firm, moved up here, and reinvented himself as a GHN honcho. Fanny turned up soon after, and he hired her at the network. We think there could be a possibility of blackmail."

"It's hard to believe that nobody at the network knew about Fanny's gender reassignment," Edwina said.

"I think the makeup woman might've figured it out," Will said. "She won't admit as much to me, but she knew more than she was saying, and she would have had a close up view of Fanny, warts and all."

"If you mean facial scars, lots of women get plastic surgery, don't they?" Edwina said.

"Yeah, but not many have their Adam's apple shaved down," Will said. "And that leaves a very particular type of scar."

"Ow," Edwina remarked, grasping her neck.

"I keep thinking about one of the cameramen I interviewed," he said. "I feel like I've seen him somewhere before, and I've been wracking my brain about it. Turns out this cameraman had a fling with Harry Crassman's ex. Harry Crassman, as in, Bobby McCloud's agent."

Edwina scrabbled around inside her backpack, and pulled out a laptop. She typed something in, and turned the screen toward Will. At the top of the page it read, 'Meet Our GHN Staff'.

"That's him," Will said, pointing to a photograph of Walter Babcock.

"Wow," Edwina replied. "This is really weird, but he looks kind of familiar to me, too."

"Listen to this," Will said, reading aloud. "'Milton started out as an actor, and appeared in several films and commercials. Many of his fans remember him as the 'Tommy's Tacos' guy'."

"Now we know why he looks familiar," Edwina said. "Let's see if he's listed in the movie data base."

A page came up for a 'Jesse Babcock'.

"There he is," she said, "younger and slimmer, but that's definitely him, and with a different first name. I guess he thought Jesse sounded better than Milton."

"Look at this," Will said. "Under 'contacts', it says 'Crassman Talent Agency'. That's Harry Crassman."

"Think he dropped Milton Babcock as a client?" she said.

"If he did, it might have ended Milton's hopes for a show biz career, and that could be the reason Milton decided to have a fling with Esther," Will said. "Classic revenge move. The suspect list goes on," he said. "There's also Mary Lou Flowers to consider—one of the other hosts. She seemed to be almost obsessively jealous of Fanny."

"Gosh, Fanny wasn't very well liked, was she?" Edwina said.

"Remember the guy I just mentioned, who embezzled from the investment firm where Fanny worked before she came to GHN? Brad Pilfer. I think it's pretty likely Fanny was blackmailing him. Mary Lou Flowers was having a clandestine affair with him. There's motive all over the place in this thing. It's possible that either of them—or both of them—were involved."

Edwina searched for a picture of Mary Lou.

"Mary Lou is old school GHN," Will said, "and Fanny was becoming more popular and successful than her—she was becoming the new face of the network. I'm pretty sure Mary Lou was lying about the reason she went to Fanny's dressing room that day. She says it was because she knew Fanny was upset about her break-up with Bobby McCloud, but I don't believe Mary Lou cared about that. She didn't care a bean about Fanny."

"Why do you think she went to Fanny's dressing room that day?" Edwina said.

"To see if the poison had worked, maybe?" Will said. "To see if she was dead? Assuming, she was involved."

"Fanny's life sounds exhausting," Edwina said. "Too much drama."

Will drained his beer.

"It would've been exhausting to a normal person, somebody with a conscience," he said. "But that wasn't Fanny. I don't think she had much of moral compass. True north for her was whatever made her feel good in the moment. She couldn't be bothered with the rules of the game—she made up her own rules as she went along."

Chapter 14

Greed has taken over the whole universe and nobody is worried about their soul.
~ Little Richard

"What?" Professor Donald Gaylord yelled into the phone. "They're cancelling the booking? You'd better be kidding about this, Manny—although, as jokes go, I have to say—it isn't remotely funny."

"What are you even talking about?" Prof. Gaylord barked shrilly at his agent. "Are you hallucinating, or something? Are you using drugs, again, Manny?"

"Of course I'm not. Let it go, Don," Manny said wearily on the other end. "It's not important. We've got other appearances lined up. Better ones. Bigger fish to fry, I'm tellin' you. I don't know why you're getting so bent out of shape about one radio interview."

"What did they say, *exactly?*" Donald pressed. "I've got to know what they actually said, word for word—and don't sugar coat it. I'm a big boy."

"C'mon, Don," Manny said. "What's the difference? That's not going to solve anything. Let's not worry about this public radio thing, okay? What can I say—they're a bunch of egghead nerds, no offense—and we don't need 'em. The book is gonna' do great. The title *alone* is genius—*Cosmic Chemistry: A Physicist's Look at Stardust.* Brilliant! You da'man, Don!"

"I swear, Manny," Donald said, "if you don't want me showing up at your office first thing tomorrow, and making a huge stink in front of the whole agency, you'll tell me right now what they said."

There was silence on the line.

"If you insist," Manny sighed. "They said it freaked them out the way you refer to yourself in the book in the third person."

More silence.

"They said you come off like a delusional narcissist."

"Lowlifes!" Donald said. "What else?"

"They weren't comfortable with Chapter Nine," Manny said.

"Chapter Nine?" Donald gasped. *"Utilizing Organic Chemistry Against Our Enemies*? What was their problem?"

"I don't know," Manny said. "They thought it was too hawkish, or something. What can you do? That's public radio for you."

Donald forced himself to take a couple of deep breaths.

"This never would have happened if my work for the NSA were official and definite," he said. "So much red tape to get through!"

"You happy now?" Manny said. "You happy you made me tell you what they said?"

"You want to know something, Manny? I think somebody got to them. Somebody who doesn't want Donald Gaylord's new book to be successful. Don't delude yourself—I've got plenty of detractors out there—mean, jealous, haters—who are just dying to see me fail.

"Do me a big favor," Donald continued. "Call those a-holes back, and tell them to forget about ever trying to book me on their show in the future! They'll live to regret this, I promise you. Donald Gaylord is a successful brand! Tell them how many followers I have on social media! Make sure they know my last book made the best seller list, for god's sake!"

"*Almost* made it," Manny muttered under his breath.

***

Professor Donald Gaylord felt badly shaken by the stinging arrows of rejection and persecution. He stood at the window of his office in Sanborn House, and gazed out across campus in an effort to calm himself. The pastoral view of pristine lawns dotted with stately, ivy-covered Georgian buildings was reminiscent of a nineteenth century landscape painting, and reminded him of his importance—reassured him of the rarefied perch he occupied in this Ivy League ivory tower. Slowly, the empty vessel of Donald Gaylord was refueling, and the cruel rejection inflicted by his tormentors at the public radio station began to ease.

Grabbing the phone from where he had thrown it across the room, he snapped a picture of himself standing by the window in front of this majestic view. He would post it later on social media where all the world, including his adversaries, could admire it.

He paced back and forth on an *aubusson* rug he had purchased from an antique shop in the French countryside, and paused in front of a mirror to remove a bit of dust from its ornate gilt frame. Beguiled by his reflection, he flicked two manicured fingers across a pair of perfectly trimmed sideburns. Straightening his tie, he grinned broadly at his image like a deranged hyena, and checked his teeth to make sure there was nothing caught in between them that might mar his splendid smile.

Public radio arseholes!

Donald popped a muscle relaxant into his mouth, and sat down at the desk. Searching quickly, he pulled up some positive reviews for his new book. Not precisely raves, there was sufficient laudatory language in them to help smooth his ruffled feathers. The combined results from the pill, and the handful of generous remarks about the book continued to calm him. He reread each positive comment aloud multiple times, as if these incantations affirmed his very existence. Now all he needed was for someone else to validate his worth, to make it real. Then, it might really be true.

***

A few doors down the hall, Edwina sat working at her desk. GHN streamed in the background on her computer at a low volume.

"I could not possibly be any more excited than I already am at this moment!" Trina Williams said with great excitement. "We have a special offer for you that only lasts until midnight tonight, and then it's gone *forever*! Please don't kick yourself tomorrow for missing out on this incredible opportunity to own this absolutely stunning set of melamine dishes and serving pieces for a lifetime of elegant, outdoor entertaining!"

Edwina took in none of this. That is to say, she experienced Trina William's chatter as a whooshing sound, like water flowing over rocks in a stream.

"Remember in the old days," Trina reminisced, "when every hostess worth her salt used her good wedding china for dinner parties? Well, the genius of the folks at 'Mamma Mia, That's Melamine?' is that they have created—exclusively for our GHN customers—a gorgeous set of dishes that combines the beauty of your good china with the practicality of your everyday dishes, and then some. It's a company that's been in business for over sixteen years, so you know they make things to last! They are the absolute iconic leaders in the industry, my friends, trust me!"

The playful set design showed a half-kitchen, half-patio motif, with an outdoor picnic table sitting on a patch of artificial grass, set with striped table linens and melamine dishes. This half of the set was surrounded by a white, picket fence and flower boxes. The interior kitchen side featured a free standing wall at the back, with a faux window dressed in gingham curtains. Trina stood at a gleaming, white countertop dropping dishes, and laughing uproariously.

"Can you imagine," Trina said, "if one of your guests at an outdoor barbeque broke a piece of your good china? O-M-G, let's not even go there! Ladies, these dishes are guaranteed to never break." She dropped another plate, and then another. They bounced without breaking off of a floor covered in an imperceptible, ultra-thin protective mat of rubber.

"What do you think of that? I'd like to see you try that with your Lenox or Spode! But seriously, you know I'm just kidding about that. Please don't drop any of your beautiful china dishes on the floor! I'm just having fun with you—you know that—hahaha!"

Absorbed as she was in thought, Edwina neither witnessed Trina's astonishing demonstration, nor noticed the knock at the door.

"Hey, kiddo," Donald Gaylord said, taking the liberty of sticking his head inside her office. "Got a minute?"

"Hey, Don," she said, looking up distractedly.

Donald closed the door behind him, and sat down across the desk from Edwina. He handed her a copy of his new book. Inside the cover was a folded print-out of a few good reviews. The inscription inside read:

To Edwina, Sic itur ad astra! With warm regards, Donald.

"Thank-you, Don, I'll look forward to reading it." she said. "Great cover. So, what can I do for you?"

"Oh, just thought I'd pop in for a quick chat," he said.

"Sure," Edwina said, wishing to return to work. "Shoot."

Donald pantomimed drawing a gun from a holster, and pointed his finger at Edwina. His accompanying laugh struck her as being alarmingly loud.

"How was the conference?" he said. "Did you get a nice crowd?"

Edwina wondered why he wouldn't have waited to have this casual conversation downstairs in the Department Library later in the day, during teatime, as he normally would have.

"Good," she said. "Good crowd on Saturday; nice reception. My paper seemed to go over reasonably well."

"That's marvelous," he replied. "Congrats, and well-deserved. Sorry I had to miss it, by the way, but the book tour's really got me tied up these days. Speaking of which, any mentions?"

Donald was most likely unaware that he was gripping the arms of the chair hard enough for his knuckles to have turned white. His legs were crossed, with the foot on the floor jiggling so insistently that his legs appeared to be keeping time to the lively compound meter of a Scottish jig.

"Mentions of your book?" Edwina said.

"Oh—you know—just wondering," he replied. "Since the book is hot off the presses, and my understanding was that the publisher would be there, touting it at the conference—I was curious, that's all. If there was any chit-chat. Doesn't matter, though," he said. "Not important!"

Edwina wished Donald weren't so needy of approbation. She didn't like being put on the spot, nor did she wish to inflame his fragile ego by saying she had not heard anyone discussing his new book during the conference. Such news was liable to be perceived by Donald as a terrible snub, and mercurial as he was, Edwina knew it might send him into a pity party—or a rage—of epic proportions, and then she would have to pick up the pieces. She wished he wouldn't ask such loaded questions.

But, to her relief—and possibly reading into her hesitation—Donald suddenly changed the subject.

"Heard you had lunch with Phil Kimby?" he said.

"Yeah, it was good to see him," Edwina said.

"So, how's the old boy doing?" Donald asked, grinning manically, baring far more teeth than looked natural.

"Pretty much the same, old Phil. In good spirits. Working hard," she said, glancing at her watch.

"Uh-huh," he replied. "Hey, what do you think of our west coast visitor this term?"

"Rachel?"

"Yeah, Rachel Driver—what a name! Suits her perfectly, don't you think? She actually looks more like a truck driver than an academic, with those tee shirts she wears, and that build of hers."

"Listen, Don, I have a class in a few minutes, so I should probably—"

"Message received!" he said, leaping from the chair, brandishing two thumbs up, and winking exaggeratedly. He had the unsettling habit of making these seemingly random, theatrical gestures that appeared to drip with significance, but Edwina could never manage to decipher what these strange pantomimes meant. Nor did she care. She was used to Donald's ways by now; he was always injecting himself into situations; always fishing. Fishing for tidbits, for gossip, for approval.

Chapter 15

We build too many walls, and not enough bridges.
                        ~ Isaac Newton

"Who can tell me why a Major League baseball player, when he hits a double, doesn't make a sharper, more efficient turn going around first on his way to second? Instead, he wastes a lot of time rounding the corner from first to second at a wide angle, which makes it more likely he'll get thrown out. Why is that?"

Edwina scanned the room.

"Yes, Polly," she said.

"Inertia?" the freshman said.

"Good," Edwina said. "Can you elaborate?"

"The law of inertia says that an object in motion—in this case the base runner—will remain in motion going in the same direction. He wouldn't be able to exert enough force on himself to make a tighter turn," Polly said.

"What would have to happen in order for him to change direction more quickly?" Edwina said.

"He would have to interact with an unbalanced force?" Polly said tentatively.

"Example? Yes, Jerrod," Edwina pointed.

"Another runner, going in a different direction?" the student replied. "Like, if an outfielder charged into the guy running from first to second, it would cause a change in his motion."

"Okay, good," Edwina replied, "Now, is this base runner of ours involved in harmonic motion?" She pointed to a student sitting in the front row.

"Derek?"

"No," Derek said. "He'd have to be oscillating back and forth around a center of equilibrium to be in harmonic motion. He's just, plain, flat-out running. There's no repeating cycle of motion running bases."

"Okay, good," Edwina said. "Now, who can give us an example of harmonic motion?"

"Stella?"

"Like, a child swinging back and forth on a swing set?" Stella said.

"Exactly like that," Edwina said. "What about this book sitting on my desk? Can we describe it in terms of inertia, even though it's not in motion?"

"Sam, go ahead," she nodded.

"Yes," he said. "Inertia also says that an object at rest will also stay at rest unless it, too, is acted upon by an unbalanced force."

"I see you've all done your reading," she said. "Excellent. *Balanced* forces are acting on that book in opposite directions right now, holding it in place, exerting equal and opposite force, right?" Edwina said. "It would require an unbalanced force to get the book to move—an applied force of some kind."

She demonstrated with a sweeping motion of her hand, knocking the book to the floor.

"Who can tell me what kind of force was working in opposition to me just then?"

"Friction?" a few students called out.

"Okay, good," Edwina nodded, glancing at the clock on the wall. "Please read the next chapter, and get to know Robert Hooke. Next time, I want everyone to bring in something that illustrates Hooke's Law. In the meantime, I want you to observe Newton's laws all throughout your day—notice which laws are in play as you're eating, getting dressed, dancing, whatever it is. Get into the habit of describing to yourself which laws are at play in any given moment, until they become second nature to you. It's actually kind of fun. It's like being privy to a secret code, or a secret language. The language of mathematics. It's what makes the world go around. Got it? See you Thursday."

***

Edwina had been looking forward to meeting up with her old thesis advisor and mentor, Nedda Cake. Now in her 90s, Professor Cake still taught a graduate seminar one day a week. As such, she and Edwina had planned to meet after Nedda's class that afternoon at Sanborn House Library, where tea and cookies were served on weekdays from four to five o'clock to students and staff in the Physics & Astronomy Department. This popular tradition had been initiated by the founder of the department, Theodore Sanborn. As stipulated in his will, Professor Sanborn had been preserved in a mahogany and glass case in which, seated in a fine suit of clothes, he was wheeled out for each and every board meeting.

The Department Library was located on the first floor of Sanborn House, just off the main entrance. It had the air of a private library in a grand country home. Antique rugs lay under genteelly worn sofas and chairs. A Georgian fireplace presided at the center of the library, surrounded by open stacks amid the carved butternut paneling. The atmosphere during teatime was relaxed and convivial.

Edwina found Nedda sitting in one of the window alcoves that ran along the west side of the library, facing the college green. The afternoon sun reflected on one side of her face as she read a newspaper. Her skin appeared almost translucent; it seemed to radiate a glow, like the silver leaf in an illuminated manuscript. Her white hair wrapped around her head in braids, and she was dressed in the usual wool skirt, blouse, and cardigan sweater.

Edwina set down two cups of tea and a small plate of cookies.

"How's your class this term?" she asked Nedda.

"Smaller than usual," Professor Cake replied. "I gather students these days are less keen on the philosophy of physics. Must be out of fashion this year. Still, they're a pretty good bunch."

"And, Honeysuckle?" Edwina said. "How's she doing?"

Nedda's middle-aged niece had moved from England to live with her when Honeysuckle's mother—Nedda's younger sister—had recently died. It seemed that Honeysuckle wasn't up to coping on her own.

"Dear Honeysuckle," Nedda sighed. "It's still an adjustment having her in the house. I wish she'd marry—or, at least, meet someone. I won't be around forever, and she does seem to need a certain amount of looking after."

"We'll have to keep thinking of someone to introduce her to," Edwina said.

"She still spends lots of time pottering around with her herbs and potions and things," Nedda continued, "which is possibly worrying, given that she insists on absolute secrecy, and won't let anyone go into the sun porch where she keeps all that stuff. But, the good news is, she gets enough translation work to keep her in pocket money. Of course, I don't charge her any rent, but I think it's important for her to be as financially independent as possible."

"I agree," Edwina said.

"I wonder if Honeysuckle thinks about inheriting the house some day? Edwina, dear, if I do happen to suddenly pop off from poisoning, you'll have your detective look into it, won't you?" Nedda said wryly. "I'm prattling. Tell me about you. How was Boston?"

"Fun," Edwina said. "The conference went well, and I was encouraged by the response."

"Good. And your lunch with Phil Kimby?" Nedda asked.

"It was great seeing him," Edwina replied. "I decided against his offer, though. I realized I don't want it on my conscience if the work ends up being appropriated for other uses. Possibly questionable to nefarious uses. It's just not worth it to me."

Nedda sipped her tea.

"I well understand your feelings," she said. "I know how much thought you must have given it—squaring the importance of the work with your own conscience. Weighing it all up. Good for you."

"I appreciate that," Edwina said. "Everyone else thinks I'm nuts."

"You're not nuts," Nedda smiled. "You're nowhere close."

Edwina laughed.

"Did you hear that Lois Leiberman is pregnant?" Edwina said. "The baby is due in June."

"Oh, that's marvelous," Nedda replied. "Lois and Seth will make wonderful parents. That child will have them wrapped around her little finger in no time. What other Department gossip have you for me?" she said.

"You know Don's doing a book tour," Edwina said. "He's been more hopped up than ever, lately—sticking his nose in everyone's business, keeping tabs on everybody."

"Poor Donald," Nedda remarked. "If only he could calm down long enough to notice that the light in his lantern is actually fire, and that his rice has been cooked all along. It's rather sad how he's forever chasing after some phantom validation that's never going to come."

"You're getting mystical in your dotage," Edwina said. "I like it."

Now it was Nedda's turn to laugh.

"How's Will?" she said. "Is he working on anything interesting?"

"As a matter of fact, he is," Edwina replied. "They're looking into a recent death at the home shopping network. You must have read about it. One of the hosts walked off the air, and dropped dead in her dressing room."

"How dreadful," Nedda muttered, biting into a cookie.

"Yes, I know," Edwina replied. "She was a young woman, so it's a bit of a mystery. I was just wondering, do you ever get to Earl's, anymore?" Edwina asked.

"No, not for a while," Nedda replied. "Why?"

"Oh," Edwina shrugged. "No special reason. Will mentioned that Earl's niece is taking over the café when Earl retires. I was just wondering if you'd met her, yet."

Nedda Cake was well acquainted with the fact that there were only a limited number of plot outlines in this life when it came to human interactions. She grasped at once the subtext behind Edwina's question.

"I wouldn't spend too much time thinking about Earl Dufresne's niece if I were you, Edwina," she said. "I gather she must be rather pretty? But, I would also take care not to take young Will for granted," the old woman said. "Not a man like Will."

Chapter 16

Pride makes us artificial and humility makes us real.
~ Thomas Merton

Dan's Bridge Market opened for business in the late 1940's in a modest farmhouse by the bridge. Rocking chairs and game tables wrapped around its deep, covered porch. Over time, Dan's had become one of New Guilford's prized institutions. As it evolved from a simple, country store into a grocery-hardware-house wares establishment, additions had been built onto the original farmhouse. Through the years of careful expansion, the rambling building had mostly managed to retain the feeling of the original structure.

When Will walked into the market that day, a familiar looking figure caught his attention. A man was hovering in front of the butcher counter, studying game sausages with great concentration, and in his hand-held basket were a head of kale, a few apples, brown sugar, an olive baguette, butter, and a bag of rice. It took Will a moment to put a name to the face; it was Jimmy Lopez—Donald Gaylord's partner. Will knew Jimmy lived in Boston, and he also knew that Donald Gaylord preferred to keep their relationship under the radar, and that Jimmy rarely, if ever, came to New Guilford as far as Will knew.

"Mr. Lopez?" Will said.

Jimmy looked up, startled.

"Will Tenney. We met last year? I interviewed you at your home in Boston during a police investigation."

Jimmy had gained weight. His boyish handsomeness, and trim, athletic build had given way to puffiness, and he looked considerably older than when Will had last seen him just over a year before.

"Of course!" Jimmy said, his face relaxing into an engaging smile. "I think I packed you up some scones, right?"

"They were delicious, by the way," Will said. "How've you been, Jimmy?"

"Oh, not too bad. Fair to middling, I guess," Jimmy said.

Jimmy's once even complexion had become mottled by a sprawl of enlarged blood vessels across his nose and cheeks. Will wondered whether the discoloration, and Jimmy's overall appearance was the result of excessive drinking.

"Things have been a little crazy," Jimmy said, his eyes welling up.

"You still living in Boston?" Will asked.

"Yes," Jimmy replied. "In the same house. I decided to drive up to New Guildford this morning on a whim. Thought I'd surprise Don with a nice, home-cooked dinner. Don hasn't been himself, lately," Jimmy said. "I don't know what's going on, but I'm actually kind of worried about him. Sorry if this is too much information, Will."

"Not at all," Will said.

"He told me he needed space," Jimmy said "but, how much space could he need? He lives up here during the week, and I'm down in Boston. We only see each other on weekends, as is it. I'd call that a pretty good amount of space, wouldn't you? He said it wasn't me; it was him—but, we've all heard that one before, right?" Jimmy laughed hollowly. "I don't know if he's having some sort of mid-life crisis, or if—— god forbid—if he might have met someone else . . ."

"It could be work related," Will said. "Is he under a lot of pressure at the college—more than usual, maybe?"

"Possibly," Jimmy said. "He's doing a book tour, and I know all the traveling is stressful. It seems like he's always complaining about something or other to do with work. I'm ashamed to say I usually tune him out when he gets going about work stuff."

Will nodded, smiling.

"It's tough only seeing each other on weekends. A million things can happen during the week, and it kind of leaves a lot of room for question marks, you know?" Jimmy said, glancing at his watch. Gosh, I'd better get going," he said. "I want to get to the house before Don does."

"Well, good luck," Will said, shaking Jimmy's hand. "It was nice to see you. I hope things work out. And if there's ever anything I can do, here's my card. Feel free to call me anytime."

***

Edwina helped herself to seconds of celery and potatoes from the roasting pan sitting in the middle of the kitchen table.

"Guess who I ran into at Dan's today?" Will said. "Jimmy Lopez."

"Really?" she said. "Jimmy's in New Guilford? That's unusual. Don is so compartmentalized about their relationship. I think Jimmy showed up at one Department Christmas party with Don—years ago— and that was the one and only time. Did you talk to him?"

"Yeah, the poor guy was pretty upset," Will said. "He said Don has cooled on their relationship, and Jimmy has no idea why. He drove up from Boston this morning hoping to smooth things over."

"Don can be very moody," Edwina asked, "Did he say anything else?"

"He said that Don's attitude toward him has changed, and that Don seems stressed out, but he won't confide in Jimmy about it, so Jimmy's thinking that Don has met someone else. He said Don's book tour might be what's stressing him out."

"I haven't heard Don complaining about it," Edwina said. "I would have thought Don was in his glory doing a book tour. He loves the attention. I feel bad for Jimmy. I hope things work out."

"Me too," Will said.

"By the way, Will," Edwina said, reaching for another piece of roasted celery, "delicious dinner!"

***

As Edwina soaked in the tub, she could hear Will moving around downstairs, making his rounds before turning in for the night. It was his habit when he stayed at her house to make sure the house was secure, that the woodstove was stoked, and that the downstairs lights were turned off.

The creaking stairs announced the completion of his nighttime rounds.

"Just got a message from Val," he said, tossing Edwina a towel as she stepped out of the tub.

"Sounds like Toby dropped some kind of bombshell. Val wants me to meet her at his office first thing in the morning."

"Any idea what it's about?" Edwina said.

"Not a clue."

Chapter 17

It is the nature of truth to struggle to the light.
~ Wilkie Collins

"You're not going to believe it," Toby said the following morning as he handed Val and Will copies of his report.

"Toxicologically speaking," he continued, "this is the most interesting case I've ever seen. The guys down at the lab are going nuts. None of us has ever seen anything like it before."

"Fanny Spendlove did not die as the result of a single toxin," he said, settling into a cracked, leather armchair behind his desk. "She died from *hundreds* of toxins that were in her system."

"Remember that pin prick between her fingers I showed you? Turns out it was a puncture wound, as I thought—but not from a needle. It was a bite mark from a tiny fang," Toby said. "A deadly little bite administered by a silent assassin of the sea. A cone snail, from the Conidae family."

Will and the Chief exchanged looks.

"May I?" Toby said, and proceeded to read aloud from an article:

"'Cone snails are marine predators that use venoms to immobilize their prey. Mainly known for their beautiful shells, their venoms contain a cocktail of peptides. Nearby fish don't stand a chance. The lethal toxins produced by these snails are in hot demand for neuroscience research, and are being developed as potent drugs. There are about thirty recorded instances of people being killed by cone snails—the mollusks are aggressive if provoked and can penetrate wetsuits with their sharp poison-loaded harpoons, which look like transparent needles. Australian scientists first separated cone snail venom into its constituent parts in 1977. Unlike most venomous animals, which produce one or a few poisons, a single snail can produce up to one hundred individual toxins'."

"My god," muttered Val. "Hell of a weapon."

"The aquarium," Will said.

"It's gotta be," said Toby. "And I can tell you this; it wasn't an accident. It couldn't have been. It takes serious planning to get hold of a cone snail, and there's no innocent reason for one of these charming little killers to take up residence in a commercial fish tank on the home shopping channel."

"So, this was an intentional poisoning," Val said.

"I'd say so," Toby replied. "Whoever put the snail in that tank as good as killed Fanny."

The office fell quiet for some moments, as Val and Will processed this unusual scenario of someone slipping a poisonous creature into a tank where any number of people could have come into contact with it, not knowing who or when the snail would strike.

"Wouldn't she have cried out, when the thing stung her?" Val said.

"Not Fanny, not on live television," Will said. "She was a pro, very ambitious, and the aquarium show was considered a big deal at GHN. If she was in pain, she would have made every effort to conceal it—to tough it out. She wouldn't have wanted to ruin such a big opportunity. Besides, wouldn't the adrenalin from being on live TV counteract the physical pain she was feeling?"

"Absolutely," said Toby, "and don't forget—she wouldn't have known the bite was lethal. So, she wouldn't necessarily have panicked, or even been afraid."

"It's such of a long shot way to kill someone, isn't it?" Val said. "Did the person who put the snail in the tank simply assume Fanny would pick it up, and that it would bite her? What are the odds of all that lining up?"

"Cone snails are known for their incredible beauty," Toby said. "She might have been drawn to it. Like we said, she wouldn't have known about its toxic properties."

"Then, wham," Toby said, hitting his fist into his other palm. "Those hypodermic teeth sank into her. She would have felt a sharp pain. And then, according to what I've read in the available literature, she would have started to feel localized numbness soon after it stung her. By the time the toxins begin to travel outward from the bite, and start to circulate through the body, you're sunk, unless you get medical help."

"So, how long would that take?" Val said.

"Again, according to what I've read, a bite from a cone snail can take place anywhere from five hours to forty minutes before death occurs, if it goes untreated," Toby said. "So, yes; I'd say the scenario of Fanny being fatally stung while she was on the air fits the time frame."

"Weirdest COD I've ever seen," the Chief muttered. "Will, see if you can get a copy of the show so we can take a look at it."

"Indeed," Toby said. "The thing I keep thinking about is how acutely aware she would have been of suffocating to death. Poor woman would have been completely conscious as she gasped for breath. Cone snail toxins don't affect the brain directly, so her mind would have been perfectly clear, and fully able to perceive exactly what was happening. Terrible way to go."

"Good lord," muttered Val.

"Take a look at this," Will said, fishing a piece of paper from his pocket. "It's a copy of Fanny's bank statement. There are quarterly cash deposits in the same amount that can't be accounted for. I think she was blackmailing Brad Pilfer."

"We know Pilfer had access to the aquarium," Will said. "He was hanging around the set that day, because of the tour group. He could've easily put the snail in the tank before Fanny went on the air, without anybody noticing. Motive and opportunity."

"Except," Val said, "blackmail victims don't usually murder their blackmailers."

"That's true," Will said, "unless their anger toward the blackmailer becomes greater that their fear of being exposed."

"You think Pilfer could be good for the murder?" Val asked.

"I'd like to say yes, but the truth is, he doesn't exactly impress me as the type to come up with such a bold plan," Will said.

"Maybe he had help. Anybody at GHN had access to the aquarium," Val said. "And, motive-wise, Mary Lou Flowers and that makeup woman look pretty good."

"And, Esther Rubenstein used to be married to Harry Crassman, don't forget—Bobby McCloud's agent. He had motive, too," Will said.

"You said something about a tour group," Val said. "We need a list of everybody who was on that tour, and their contact information. We need to talk to all of them. Would they have had access to the aquarium, do you think?"

"Possibly," Will said, making notes. "I'll find out."

"And find out if the aquarium was secured before Fanny's show—or was it sitting somewhere backstage, out in the open where anybody could get to it?" Val said. "And see if you can scare Pilfer, while you're at it. He's holding out on us."

***

Later that day, Will and Val reviewed a tape of Fanny's last show in Val's office.

"There it is," Val said. "See that? That's when the thing bit her, right there. Fanny picks something up out of the tank and either it slipped—or she dropped it—back in the water."

"Man," Will said, "she barely reacted."

"Well, like you said," Val replied, "Fanny was a pro."

***

"May I speak with Amaleen Stuckey, please?" Will said.

"This is Amaleen," replied the voice at the other end.

"This is William Tenney. I'm a detective with the New Guilford Police Department in New Hampshire, and we're contacting everyone who was on the recent tour at the GHN home shopping network. Do you mind answering a few questions?"

"Sure," Amaleen said. "What's this about?"

"Nothing to be nervous about, ma'am," he replied. "We're just gathering information—routine procedure in a situation like this. One of the hosts at the network died on the day of the studio tour." Will said. "Were you aware of that?"

"What in the world?" she said. "No—I—no. I didn't know anything about that."

"Do you happen to know anyone personally employed at GHN? Did you know Fanny Spendlove, or have any type of relationship with her?"

"Fanny Spendlove is dead?" Amaleen repeated.

"Yes, ma'am," Will said. "She was killed. Were you personally acquainted with her?"

"Well, no," Amaleen stammered. "I didn't actually know her, but I did call into the show a few times, the way people do, and I might've talked to her on the phone once or twice. I've spoken with quite a few of the hosts over the years. It's how I do most of my shopping."

"So," Will said, "I take it you're a GHN regular—a big fan?"

"Yes," Amaleen said, looking around her apartment. "But it wasn't my idea to make a trip up there. My friend, Connie, won two tickets in a contest, and she invited me to come along."

"Have you had contact with any GHN employees other than the times you called into the station?" he said.

"Depends on what you mean by 'contact'," she said.

"Were you in communication at any time with anyone who worked at GHN?"

"If you call posting messages on some of the hosts' personal pages being 'in contact', then I guess I was," she said.

"And the times you called in, were you speaking live on the air, or were some of them private calls?" Will asked.

Ouch. Amaleen winced at the memory of having such high hopes of talking to Fanny in private.

"No private calls, just on the air," Amaleen said.

"The day you went on the tour, did anyone approach you at any time? Was there anything, or anyone, that seemed strange or out of place that day?"

"Like what?" Amaleen replied.

"Like anything, Miss Stuckey. Anything at all that might have struck you as odd, or someone who looked suspicious, or like they shouldn't be there."

"No, nothing I can think of," Amaleen answered.

"Did you leave the tour group at any point?" Will said. "Was there any time you were by yourself?"

"Not really," Amaleen replied. "Just the one time when I had to use the little girls' room."

"How long were you away from the group?"

"Not more than five minutes, Detective. I'm sure that's all it was."

"Well," Will said, "if you think of anything else, no matter how small or unimportant it might seem, please get in touch with me. Sometimes people remember little things later on, things that turn out to be really helpful with our investigation."

"Detective?"

"Yes?"

"Can I ask you how Fanny died?"

"She was poisoned," Will said.

"Poisoned? Oh my goodness, that's awful," she said.

"Thank-you for speaking with me, ma'am. We'll get in touch again if need be. Good-bye."

When the call was over, Amaleen felt unsettled, and sick to her stomach. She paced along the worn pathways in the carpeting around her apartment. Even though it was only late afternoon, she decided to take to her bed for the rest of the day with a box of Mabel's Macaroon Meltaways (GHN, $8.98; second box for only $6.98). After eating a few of these coconut confections, the sugar high felt good, but did little to allay her anxiety. *We'll get in touch again if need be?* Amaleen hoped there wouldn't be any reason for that.

***

Will's phone rang as he was leaving the station that evening.

"Hello, Will? It's Jimmy Lopez."

"Hi, Jimmy. How are you?"

"Well, my conscience has been bothering me," Jimmy said.

Excellent, thought Will. *I like it when peoples' consciences bother them.*

"What can I do for you, Jimmy?"

"I found something out last night when I confronted Donald, and I didn't want to leave town without calling you."

"Uh-huh," Will said.

"Not that it has anything to do with that woman's death at the home-shopping station," Jimmy said, "but I thought it might be of use to you. Like I said," Jimmy continued, "I kind of had it out with Donald last night. I just couldn't take not knowing what was going on, anymore. With us, I mean. Wondering if we were going to split up, if he'd met someone else . ."

"So, it turns out Donald knew the dead woman— back in the day—and that's what's been putting him on edge." he said.

"Oh?" Will said.

"Yes. Donald knew her before she had sexual reassignment surgery. He told me they had a fling years ago, before—you know—before she became 'Fanny'."

"This is very helpful, Jimmy. I really appreciate the information," Will said.

"So, understandably," Jimmy said, "Donald was completely freaked out when she turned up dead. He was worried his connection with her might come out, and that it would hurt his reputation, or that he might even get caught up in the investigation. That's why he's been so distant with me, lately. He's been worried sick about the whole thing."

"Of course," Will said. "Totally understandable."

"I did everything I could think of to reassure him, but the poor man still feels pretty wretched," Jimmy said. "At least he felt a little bit better once he got it off his chest, but it's obvious that her death stirred up some bad memories for him."

"How so?"

"Well," Jimmy said, "let's just say Donald had a number of one-night stands in his younger days. He was a bit wild. I think he feels ashamed of that part of his life. And Fanny reminded him of all that."

"How did he find out that Fanny Spendlove used to be Gus Prestopino?" Will asked.

"From what I understand," Jimmy said, "it was Fanny who got in touch with Donald. She emailed him, and told him who she was, and how she was working nearby at GHN, etcetera. She wanted to get together, but Donald refused."

"Do you think Fanny could have been blackmailing him?" Will asked.

"I never thought of it," Jimmy said, "and Don didn't mention anything like that."

Will paused, waiting for Jimmy to do the math. If Fanny had been blackmailing Donald, threatening to go public with their past relationship, Donald would have a good motive for her murder.

"Not sure I like where you're going with this, Will," he said.

"I have to look at everything, Jimmy," Will replied. "It's nothing personal."

Val Burnstein had already left for the day. Will sent her a text.

Jimmy Lopez just called me. Gaylord was sexually involved with Fanny Spendlove years ago when she was Gus Prestopino. Fanny might've been blackmailing him. I will talk to Gaylord right after I see Pilfer tomorrow.

Chapter 18

*Oh what a tangled web we weave/When first we
practice to deceive.*
~ Sir Walter Scott

Despite GHN's fervent disclaimer about the freak
nature of Fanny's accidental poisoning, damage control
fell woefully short. New orders for aquariums halted,
and those customers who had already placed orders
called frantically to cancel them, and demand refunds.
Sales across the board at the network were suffering
from a sharp decline in consumer confidence.
Management had never seen anything like it. Even the
notorious recall a few years earlier of a popular set of
artificial Christmas tree candles, due to fire hazard, did
not compare to the current debacle. A feeling of near
hysteria shrouded the place all the way from purchasing
to corporate. The legal department teetered daily on the
brink of all-out panic. Warehouse activity ground to a
halt, and fork lift operators and loaders showed up for
work with little to do other than talk about Fanny's
death.

And yet, there was something inexplicably
invigorating about the recent tragedy. There seemed to
be nothing quite like an untimely and suspicious death
to make people come alive, and to spark a sense of
solidarity among them, and create the illusion of
connectedness. In the days following the accident, the
GHN family grew closer as they buzzed with ghoulish
interest and speculation, and there emerged from the

collective *schadenfreude* a spirit of corporate bonhomie. It was amidst this curious atmosphere that Will returned to interview VP Brad Pilfer.

The phone lines rang so continuously in Mr. Pilfer's office that Will asked him to shut it off. At best, VP Pilfer seemed distracted; at worst, he was fighting back a nervous breakdown.

"Sorry about all the hubbub," the GHN exec said, his complexion trending a gray-green. "Things are pretty crazy around here at the moment, as you can see."

"Thanks for seeing me under the circumstances," Will said, "I had some follow up questions I wanted to ask you.

"Whatever I can do to help, Detective."

"We discovered a trail of regular payments in Fanny's bank records that we can't account for. Any idea what those might be?"

Radio silence.

"Was Fanny blackmailing you?" Will asked.

"Blackmailing me?" Mr. Pilfer said. His eyes darted around the room, as if he were searching for a teleprompter to feed him his next line.

"Oh, Christ," he muttered. "It was stupid of me. I might as well tell you, because you're bound to find out. I agreed to pay Fanny to keep quiet about what happened back in New York—at McAndrews Larsen— it all happened such a long time ago, but she just wouldn't let go of it. I take it you already know about that?"

"Yes, sir."

"I figured it would come out," Pilfer said. "First, she demanded that I hire her here at GHN, and after that it was money."

Will sat tight, waiting for the implication of this statement to dawn on Mr. Pilfer.

"But I didn't kill her!" he said. "Oh my god, is that what you think? Honest to god, I didn't kill her! I mean, I could have moved away from the area, gotten another job if I wanted to—I would never kill anyone! I'm much too spineless for that—just ask my wife. And besides, I wasn't the only person around here who had issues with Fanny—believe me; you don't have to look very far."

"Like who, for instance?" Will said.

"The make-up woman, for one," he replied, a rush of color brightening his face. "That vindictive little troll, Esther Rubenstein. She couldn't stand Fanny. I think the phrase she liked to use was 'vulgar upstart'.

"Not to mention half the hosts who also couldn't stand Fanny, either. Listen, Detective, I know it's wrong to speak ill of the dead, but the truth is, Fanny was too ambitious for her own good, and she rubbed a lot of people the wrong way. I wouldn't be a bit surprised if she was extorting money from other people besides me. She was always working some kind of angle."

Will regarded V.P. Pilfer coolly. Some people just can't get off the hot seat fast enough.

"What makes you say that, Mr. Pilfer?"

"Well, I can tell you for a fact that Mary Lou Flowers mentioned seeing an envelope stuffed with cash in Fanny's dressing room on more than one occasion," he said.

"Just lying out in the open?" Will said.

"Well," Mr. Pilfer replied, "possibly it was inside Fanny's purse. I'm not really sure of the details. I'll tell you something else interesting," the VP said, happy to be of help by throwing other people under the bus, "most of the gals around here wear GHN gemstone jewelry—which is to say, fake stuff. Our gemstone products are very realistic, and most people can't tell the difference. Even with the diamonds. But not Fanny. Her jewelry was the real McCoy, stuff she couldn't possibly have afforded on her salary. She had extra income coming in from somewhere, that's for sure—I mean, besides what she was getting from me. I once saw her flashing around an emerald ring that must've cost a fortune. Definitely the real deal, and she made sure everybody knew it, too."

"Did she wear this expensive jewelry on the air?" Will asked.

"She might have," said Mr. Pilfer. "There's no written policy here against wearing personal jewelry on the air, as such, although we discourage it."

"Why is that?" Will inquired.

"For the most part, we require our hosts to wear GHN merchandise on the air, because modeling the items we sell naturally helps with sales—but it's also because our viewers don't like it when the hosts wear their own jewelry or clothing or hair accessories—items that are not available for sale at GHN. We've had lots of feedback about it over the years. Complaints, actually. Our brand is 'gotta have it now', don't forget, and we take that seriously. If our viewers see something they want, our job is to make sure they get it."

"Why do you ask if Fanny wore her jewelry on the air, anyway?" Mr. Pilfer asked.

"If somebody watching GHN knew her jewelry was real," Will said, "they might have become jealous, or resentful, or curious about how she came by such expensive pieces. Something along those lines might point to motive."

"Yes, I see. Fanny had a knack for rubbing people the wrong way, and that's putting it mildly," Mr. Pilfer said. "I'm sorry to say, I think there were quite a few people who weren't especially sorry to see her go."

Will soon took his leave, reflecting on the fact that he could not recall disliking a person so much, so quickly, as Brad Pilfer.

***

On his way down in the elevator, Will got a text from Val.

Put a priority on Neptune Aquatics, get up there when you finish with Pilfer.

He checked his watch, and headed north on the highway.

Forty-five minutes later, Will pulled into Neptune Aquatics, where a man whom he took to be the owner was waiting in the parking lot. C. J. Waterman approached Will's car with a look of worry, and an air of forlorn vulnerability, carrying a folder under his arm.

"Please understand," he said, fixing Will with watery, imploring eyes, "I've been in this business for thirty-two years, and nothing like this has ever happened before. Nobody in their right mind would ever stock a cone snail, let alone put one in a commercial tank. It's all very distressing." The sad, wispy man looked as if he might blow over in the breeze.

Will opened the folder. It contained the documented transactions between Neptune Aquatics and GHN, including a signed receipt for the aquarium Fanny presented on the day it arrived at GHN. The contents of the tank were itemized, right down to the exact weights and amounts of polished pebbles and decorative rocks. No cone snail was listed anywhere.

"Thank-you. This all looks in very good order, Mr. Waterman," Will said. "Any idea how this might have happened? How a cone snail might have found its way into your aquarium?"

"None at all," the man replied, his face ashen. "It's absolutely terrible. Who would do such a thing? I feel just awful for that poor girl and her family."

"How would someone go about getting their hands on a cone snail?" Will said. "Would it be difficult?"

"Oh, my goodness," Mr. Waterman said, looking stricken by the very thought of it.

"I suppose you could travel to someplace like Hawaii to acquire one, and then ship it back," Mr. Waterman said. "Another way might be to buy one over the internet. I'm sorry to say, some dealers aren't very scrupulous about exporting dangerous animals, you know—they'll do anything for money. It's just a business to them."

"That's very helpful, sir," Will said, jotting down notes. "I wonder if I might speak to whoever it was that physically delivered the aquarium to GHN?"

"Yes, of course," Mr. Waterman said, ushering Will inside the nondescript, industrial building, and into his office. A handsome aquarium stood in the middle of the room, artfully lit to showcase the silent world of inhabitants gliding gracefully through miniature castles and grottos.

"Lorraine," Mr. Waterman said into the intercom, "please have Sammy and Miguel come to my office."

Moments later, two neatly dressed young men appeared in his office.

"Yes, Mr. Waterman?"

"Please, sit down, fellas," Mr. Waterman said. "The detective here just wants to ask you some questions about the delivery to GHN. Nothing to be nervous about. Nothing at all. I promise."

It didn't take long for Will to rule out the possibility that either young man knew anything about the cone snail. Each was forthcoming and open, at ease answering all his questions.

"These are very fine, hard-working, men, detective," C. J. Waterman said. "I can assure you of their good character, and I can vouch for their honesty one hundred percent."

***

"My god," Mr. Waterman said as he walked Will back to his car, "who would think to put a poisonous creature in a tank designed for home use, where there are children and babies and pets? It boggles the mind. Very distressing."

"We'll find him, sir," Will said, shaking Mr. Waterman's hand. "I'll keep you posted. In the meantime, here's my card. Please feel free to call me anytime."

C. J. Waterman lingered, staring forlornly at the clouds. Will watched him in his rear view mirror as he exited the parking lot of Neptune Aquatics.

Will pulled onto the interstate, and headed back to New Guilford, thinking about Mr. Waterman's question: what sort of person would use an exotic sea creature as a weapon for murder? Someone creative, someone with imagination. Getting hold of a cone snail in the first place showed a certain amount of resourcefulness and planning. Did the choice of weapon have some secret meaning? Was there a private message in it? Or, was it chosen opportunistically, tailored to fit in with the circumstance of Fanny selling a fish tank? Occupied with this line of thinking, Will arrived at the Cushing campus in what felt like no time at all.

***

Reflexively, he glanced around for Edwina as he trotted up the staircase at Sanborn House. He turned left on the second floor landing, and found Donald Gaylord's office halfway down the long hallway. He knocked.

"Yes? Come in," Professor Gaylord called through the closed door.

Donald Gaylord's office presented a stark contrast to Edwina's, which was comfy and inviting, and considerably smaller. The self-important furnishings in Professor Gaylord's office reminded Will of a fusty, roped off period room in a museum that had bored him senseless as a child, where you were allowed to look but not touch. Prof. Gaylord's office felt equally forbidding.

"Nice to see you again, Detective Tenney," Donald Gaylord said from behind his desk. "Please, have a seat."

This was easier said than done. Will took a quick inventory of his options. It would either have to be a Louis XV rococo settee, upholstered in striped silk, or a petite 18th C. fruitwood armchair that looked as if it might collapse under his weight. Will opted for the settee.

"What can I do for you?" Donald said genially.

"Just wanted to follow up with you on a few things," Will said. "We know now that Fanny was making regular bank deposits that well exceeded the amount of her salary. We've been able to account for the source of some of these funds, but not all of them. I was wondering if you had any ideas?"

"Why ask me?" Donald replied pleasantly. "I didn't even know the woman."

Will had decided beforehand that he would not bring Jimmy Lopez into the conversation. Naming Jimmy as a source of information would put Jimmy in an untenable position, and Will wanted to protect Jimmy from possible repercussions. Under the circumstances, lying was a much better option.

"We know that Fanny underwent sexual reassignment surgery at some point," Will said. "The name on her birth certificate is 'Gus Prestopino'."

Donald's jaw muscles clenched and unclenched several times, just the sort of reaction Will was looking for.

"Sorry to be indelicate, sir," Will improvised, "but we found a notebook—kind of a diary, actually—that belonged to Fanny. Your name appears in an entry from years ago, when she was living as Gus Prestopino."

Will and Donald stared expressionlessly at one another for a few moments as the latter composed his response. When Donald suddenly exploded into laughter, Will was caught off guard.

"What was it Oscar Wilde said?" Donald said. "That, 'experience is simply the name we give our mistakes'? Well, Detective Tenney, my brief encounter with Gus was an interesting experience! It happened a hell of a long time ago, and I barely remember it. In fact, I'm ashamed to say I only vaguely remember the name, 'Gus', and beyond that detail, I hardly remember anything else," Donald said. "I'm afraid I was a naughty boy in those days, guilty of any number of youthful indiscretions. A genuine 'love-em-and-leave-em' type, don't you know. Happily, I'm now older and wiser."

Will regarded Donald with a neutral expression.

"Well, I'll be! So, you're telling me that Gus transformed himself into a television salesgirl?" Donald said. "How extraordinary!"

"So it seems," Will said. "Had you had any contact with Fanny?"

"Of course not," Donald said. "Look around you, man! Do you imagine I shop from a television department store? Or that I would revisit a relationship––if you can call it that—I hardly remember?"

"Kind of a coincidence, though, isn't it," Will said, "that Fanny would pop up living so nearby? We know for certain she was blackmailing someone."

"Really? Well, it wasn't me," Donald said. "You know as well as I do this area attracts people from all over the world. It's quite a stretch to think that this person I barely even know, decided to move near me after all these years. I'm afraid you'll have to do better than this random fishing expedition. Sorry to disappoint."

Donald hadn't taken the bait. Will's effort to flush out an admission from Donald that he had been in recent touch with Fanny had stalled. Was Donald lying about it out of guilt or embarrassment? Did he have something to do with Fanny's death, or was he hiding his association with her simply in order to keep his name out of the investigation?

Chapter 19

*Logic will get you from A to B. Imagination will take
you everywhere.*
~ Albert Einstein

"I'm going to do some work later," she said over her
shoulder as she washed dishes in the sink. "Make mine
caffeinated, please. You staying over?"

"Can't tonight. I told Cyrus I'd show him how to use
my copper cutter; he wants to borrow it this weekend,
so I'll need to head out pretty soon. Besides, I'm getting
up really early to drive to New York in the morning."

"Oh, right," Edwina said.

"Meant to tell you, I heard from Jimmy Lopez
again," Will said.

"What'd he say?"

"Apparently Don Gaylord, knew—and by 'knew', I
mean slept with—Fanny Spendlove years ago, before
her reassignment surgery. Back when she was Gus
Prestopino."

Edwina turned around to face him. A wet plate
dripped soapy water onto the floor.

"Wow," she uttered.

"Yup. Don told Jimmy all about it the other night.
They finally had it out, and Jimmy got to the bottom of
why Don was acting so distant and weird. Don told him
that he had known Fanny a long time ago, before she
was Fanny, and before Don ever met Jimmy, and that
Fanny's death was freaking him out because he was

afraid his connection with her might come out in the course of the investigation, and hurt his reputation."

She dried her hands on a dish towel, and picked up the cup of tea Will had made for her.

"That sounds like Don," she said. "He's obsessed with his career and his standing in the academic community, but I don't think he'd kill anybody over it. It's just too far-fetched. When did all this happen, anyway? With Don and Gus Prestopino?" Edwina asked.

"According to Jimmy, it happened when Don was a grad student, during some wild weekend at a symposium in San Francisco."

***

Edwina sat down to work after Will left, but their earlier exchange kept playing in her mind, and made it difficult for her to think about anything other than the possibility of Donald Gaylord being a murderer. Somebody she had studied with, and worked alongside for years. It didn't seem possible.

The house was dead quiet, except for the occasional whistle of sap popping in the fire every now and then. Edwina got up to make another cup of tea. While she waited for the kettle to boil, she rooted around in the cupboards for something sweet. All she could find was an unfamiliar-looking package of cookies with an overdue sell-by date. When she tried to coax one from the plastic packaging, it crumbled into cookie dust, and she tossed the whole thing away.

She sat back down at the kitchen table, pushed her work aside, and sipped the hot, milky tea. She let her mind drift into a sort of dream state where ideas came and went without being edited or deleted. It was like daydreaming, except she didn't choose what to think about. She let the thoughts pick her. It was a way of finding out what was rattling around in there. Any number of seemingly random images, snippets of conversations, and thoughts began to float around in her head.

Phillip Kimby was one of them. Her old colleague had expressed interest in the Fanny Spendlove investigation during their lunch in Boston. He had asked quite a few questions about it, hadn't he? What was his interest in it? Did he know something about this whole business? Phillip was a broker of secrets—no question about that—a dealer in information. But, what could his connection be to the investigation? Fanny did seem to have far-reaching tentacles, but how and why would she and Phil Kimby possibly have crossed paths? It would likely turn out that Phil had no connection at all to the case.

Chapter 20

*A man of such obvious and exemplary charm must be a
liar.*
~ Anita Brookner

Bobby McCloud's production company occupied a
rarefied piece of New York City real estate. The offices
were housed in a handsome carriage house located in a
gated, Greenwich Village mews, part of a row of
carriage houses that had been built in the nineteenth
century as stables for the neighboring townhouses.
These carriage houses had been converted into artists'
studios in the early twentieth century. And, before that,
the land belonged to a large, eighteenth century farm.
Will lingered for a few minutes, gazing at the
architecture, and trying to imagine the buildings and
property in their earlier incarnations.

Slight of build, Bobby McCloud was surprisingly
delicate looking in person, far from the stalwart action
figure he appeared to be on screen. He looked
considerably older than his late twenties, too, even
careworn. The things movie lighting and camera angles
could do!

"Hey, man," Bobby said, displaying the trademark
crooked smile that telegraphed his bad boy charm.
"What can I get you? Espresso? Tea? Sparkling water?
How about some lunch—have you eaten?"

"Nothing, thanks," Will said, taking a seat on a
leather sofa. The office had been impeccably appointed
at great expense to achieve a restrained, minimalist

look. Sunshine streamed in through a bank of windows, bathing the sculptural furnishings and modern artwork in natural lighting. A commercial, Italian espresso machine with polished spigots sat atop a mahogany bar.

Bobby perched on the corner of a massive, glass desk with stainless steel seams, where five cell phones were lined up within easy reach.

"Thank-you for agreeing to see me, Mr. McCloud," Will said.

"My pleasure," Bobby replied. "Anything to help."

"We are investigating the death of Fanny Spendlove, and I understand you knew her, is that right?"

"Absolutely," the actor replied with practiced charm, running his fingers through thick, highlighted hair. "Fanny and I were very good friends, as I guess you already know. It's such a tragedy, her death. I can hardly believe it's true. Can I ask you how she died? It hasn't been reported, yet."

"She was poisoned," Will replied.

"Wow, that's awful," Bobby said. "That is just—so––completely horrible."

"Can you tell me a little bit about your relationship, if you don't mind?" Will asked.

"Absolutely, anything I can do, like I said," Bobby said amiably, sipping espresso from a porcelain demitasse. "Fanny and I were seeing each other for about six or seven months. It was a casual thing on my part—not to sound like a total jerk—but I think it might have been a little more serious on her end. Anyway, my agent didn't like Fanny very much, so I broke it off."

"Your agent didn't like her?" Will repeated.

"Yeah."

"Harry Crassman?" Will said.

"Yup. Harry's my guy."

"So, you broke off your affair with Fanny because Harry Crassman didn't much care for her. Why was that?" Will asked.

"You know how it is," Bobby shrugged, smiling. "It's kind of—"

He was interrupted by a ringing phone, which he scooped up quickly, and headed into the hallway outside his office.

"Sorry," he said to Will, "this will only take a second."

Will took the opportunity to look around the office. He glanced at the covers of the magazines and trade publications that lay neatly fanned out on the coffee table. Bobby McCloud looked up at him from the cover of *People* magazine, dated a few months earlier. The caption read, *Adopted at Birth—Finally Feeling Secure After Years of Success.*

"Sorry about that—so, where were we?" Bobby said when he reappeared moments later.

"You were going to tell me why Harry Crassman didn't like Fanny," Will said, "and why his opinion mattered so much that you ended your relationship with her."

"Right, right," Bobby said genially. "The thing is, Will, there's been some unfavorable press about me over the years. Comes with the territory; you know what I mean. It's mostly the tabloids, which I don't personally pay any attention to, but Harry is very sensitive about these things. He's very protective of me." Bobby paused to take a sip of espresso.

"I started in the business young—as a kid—and Harry has always been kind of like a second father to me. Or, maybe I should say *third* father," Bobby laughed. "There's my bio dad—whoever that might be--then there's my adoptive dad, and then there's good old Harry."

"I just recently decided to open up to the public about my childhood," Bobby said. "Harry thought it would be good for my career. Don't know if you happened to see the story in *People?*"

"I was just looking at it," Will said, nodding toward the magazines on the table. "Must have been tough to open up like that."

"So, to answer your question," Bobby said, "when it came to Fanny, I guess maybe Harry was a little bit of a snob. He didn't think it was good for the Bobby McCloud brand to be dating somebody who makes her living selling *tchotchkes* on TV."

"Uh-huh," Will said.

"Plus, you have to understand, I've already been married a couple of times, and each divorce sets me back a bundle, and that's money that comes out of Harry's pocket, too," Bobby said. "He thought Fanny was after a paycheck."

This time they were interrupted by a different phone. Bobby picked it up, and quickly retreated once again into the hallway, with a wink in Will's direction. Will sidled toward the door to see if he could hear anything, but only managed to make out the repeatedly used words 'baby' and 'sorry'.

"My apologies, Will; I had to take that call," Bobby said when he came back in.

"No worries," said Will. "You're a busy man, and I won't take up much more of your time. We were talking about Harry's attitude toward Fanny."

"Right," Bobby said. "So, one day Harry said to me, 'Kid, this girl is trouble. She'll end up suing you for breach of promise, or some bullshit like that. She'll drag our asses into court, and it'll end up costing us a bundle.' That was the gist of it, anyway, and Harry's the boss".

"How did you and Fanny happen to meet in the first place?" Will asked.

"She attended the opening night party for one of my movies," Bobby replied. "She works—excuse me," he shook his head, "*worked*—with Jonny Billious, the celebrity chef. GHN sells Jonny's stuff—pots and pans, I guess, and stuff like that. This particular party was at Jonny's downtown restaurant, and Fanny was there, plus a few of the GHN suits. It might have been Jonny who introduced us, although I'm not positive about that. I started seeing Fanny soon after the party, maybe a week or two later."

"Did the relationship become sexual right away, or——"

"Yeah," Bobby said.

"Where did you and Fanny usually see one another?" Will said. "Here in New York?"

"Yeah. Fanny came down to the city on business every so often. We'd go out for dinner, and she'd stay at my place. Again, not to sound like a bad guy, but it was a pretty casual thing on my end. I guess maybe not so much for her, though. You're a good looking guy, Will—you know the drill; am I right?"

"Fanny was a television sales personality, and you're a big celebrity," Will said. "Did you really think she would take a casual attitude toward the relationship?"

"Yeah, you're probably right," Bobby shrugged. "Harry said the same thing. He told me she had photos of me plastered up on her website. He insisted she take them down."

"When did you decide to break things off with her?" Will said.

Bobby's eyes welled up with tears. Will wasn't sure if he was acting or not. He wondered if Bobby, himself, even knew.

"That's the thing," Bobby said. "I tried to break it off with her on the phone a few weeks ago, but she freaked out. She started calling and texting me, day and night after that. Pleading with me to give the relationship another shot."

"Did Harry Crassman know about all of that?"

"Oh, sure," Bobby replied. "My life's an open book to Harry. It was his idea for me to call it quits with Fanny over the phone, instead of face to face, in case there was some kind of scene. You know, the kind of crap the tabloids are always trying to get a piece of."

"What did Harry tell you to do when you told him Fanny wouldn't take no for an answer?" Will said.

"He basically said, you know, just let her down easy. Stay non-committal. Try to lessen contact little by little—get my contact numbers changed—become unavailable 'til she gets the message."

"How did that go?" Will said. "Sounds like she was trying to hang onto you any way she could."

"It was rough-going," Bobby said. "Harry was pretty worried there, for a while. Wait a second—you don't think Harry had anything to do with Fanny's death, do you?" Bobby said.

"Or *me,* for chrissakes? I mean—yeah—Harry gets into fights with people sometimes. You've probably heard he's been arrested for throwing a few punches over the years. He can be pretty aggressive and moody––I think he might be bipolar or something—but he's basically a good guy."

"So, did Harry's advice work?" Will asked.

"More or less," Bobby replied. "I felt bad about having to keep ducking her like that, but...."

"When was the last time you saw Fanny?" Will asked.

"I don't remember exactly," Bobby said. "My assistant will probably have a record of it. You can check with her on your way out."

If Bobby was dropping a hint that the meeting was finished, Will ignored it.

"Where do you live?" Will said.

"I have a townhouse on the upper east side," Bobby answered.

"Is that your only residence?" Will said.

"I have a place in LA, and I have a house near Exmouth."

"Exmouth?" Will said.

"West coast of Australia," Bobby replied. "I only wish I had more time to spend out there. It's the most incredible—unbelievably beautiful. I go scuba diving with my dog whenever I'm lucky enough to get some time off."

"You go scuba diving with your dog?" Will repeated, not knowing if Bobby were joking or not.

"Oh, yeah," Bobby replied. "They make this totally adorable scuba gear for dogs these days. It's a blast. Orson loves it."

"When were you last in Australia?" Will asked.

"Let's see," Bobby said, "must have been—oh, right, I remember. I was there about a month and a half ago, for about a week. Again, feel free to get exact dates from my assistant."

"Did Fanny go with you?"

"No. I wanted her to, but Harry nixed it," Bobby said.

"I understand there are cone snails in that part of the world," Will said. "Ever seen one?"

"Oh, sure," Bobby said. "It's not just sharks you have to watch out for. You've got to be able to recognize all kinds of poisonous things if you want to avoid getting into trouble. There are some crazy, deadly predators in Australia."

Some crazy, deadly predators here, too, thought Will. *They're just harder to identify.*

"Why do you ask about cone snails?" said Bobby, finger combing a lock of hair back from his forehead.

"Fanny died from cone snail poisoning," Will replied.

"You're kidding, right?" Bobby said.

"I wish I were," Will said.

"But that's—that's so insane!" Bobby said. "How could that be? How would Fanny come into contact with a cone snail—it doesn't even make sense."

"It actually happened when she was on the air," Will said. "She was bitten by a cone snail during the presentation of a saltwater aquarium. Thousands of viewers would have seen it, without realizing what had happened. We're trying to find out who was responsible for putting it in the tank. That's why we need to ask everyone who knew her where they were in the last few days."

"Of course," Bobby said. "I understand completely. God, how awful! Poor Fanny!"

"Did you ever visit Fanny in New Hampshire?"

"Nah," Bobby said, "She wanted me to, but I never made it up there."

"Had you planned to?" Will said.

"No," Bobby said, "not really."

"Do you own an aquarium, yourself?" Will asked.

"Yes, I do," Bobby replied. "The designer Harry hired to decorate my townhouse thought an aquarium would look great in the library, so he had one installed. I don't maintain the thing, myself—I have somebody who comes in to do that. Harry found him."

"I'd like the person's contact information, if you don't mind," Will said. "The person who looks after your aquarium."

"Of course," Bobby replied. "Just ask Stephanie on your way out."

"Do you know if there are any cone snails in your aquarium?" Will asked.

"No way," Bobby said. "I can't think of any reason why somebody would keep cone snails in a domestic aquarium. They're way too dangerous."

"One more thing, for the time being," Will said. "Did you know Fanny had undergone gender reassignment surgery?"

Bobby grimaced.

"I didn't know it at the time," he said, "but I found out later."

"Didn't know it at the time of what?" Will said.

"God, this is really embarrassing," Bobby said. "During the time we were sleeping together, I—I did not know—I couldn't tell—that Fanny had had surgery. I didn't find out until later."

"How did you find out?" Will said.

"Harry did some digging around. He didn't like Fanny—didn't trust her from the get-go. I guess he wanted to have something on her in case she tried to get money out of me down the road. He found out about her sex-change. He went pretty nuts, actually. Thought it could end my career if it ever came out."

"How'd you feel when you found out about it?" Will said.

"Embarrassed. Disgusted. Sick to my stomach. Betrayed," Bobby said. "Probably the same as you'd feel."

"Were you angry at Fanny?"

"Wouldn't you be?" Bobby said. "I felt like an idiot. I was livid. But I didn't hurt her, if that's where we're going. That's not my style, Will."

"Did Fanny ever talk to you about her work?" Will said.

"Yeah, she talked about it sometimes," Bobby answered. "She really got going about it if she'd been drinking. About how cutthroat her business was, and how competitive. She was pretty ambitious, you know. She wanted to be top dog at that network. I think she had ideas about getting her own clothing line, or skin care, or something—I forget, exactly."

"Uh-huh. Did she ever mention anyone in particular she didn't get along with at the network? Maybe someone she especially disliked?" Will asked.

"Hm . . . not that I can think of," Bobby said. "Wait a second. There was one guy Fanny complained about a few times. One of the execs."

"Why didn't she like him?" Will said.

"Sorry, I can't remember the reason," Bobby said.

"Got a name?" Will said.

"Oh, man," Bobby said, squinting at the ceiling. "It was something like—Chad—Silver?"

Will flipped through his notes.

"Brad Pilfer?" he said.

"That's the guy," Bobby said, flashing his million dollar smile.

***

Will stepped out of the elevator on the twenty-fifth floor of a mid-town office building, and pushed open a set of heavy glass doors marked 'Crassman Talent Agency, New York-Los Angeles-London'. The reception area was decorated with sleek, pale gray leather chairs and potted palm trees in concrete containers. A well dressed woman of indeterminate age sat behind the desk wearing a headset. She looked up.

"Detective Tenney to see Mr. Crassman," he said.

"He's expecting you," she said. "Can I get you anything? Sparkling water; coffee?"

"No, thank-you," Will replied.

Floor-to-ceiling windows in Harry's impressive office overlooked the busy neighborhood. A pair of curved sofas flanked a marble coffee table. The low table was covered—just as in Bobby's office—with trade papers and magazines. Harry Crassman sprang up from behind a massive desk, and bounded across the office to greet Will.

"Sit, sit!" Harry said, shaking Will's hand firmly.

"Such news about Fanny! Killed by a snail, my god!" he said.

"How did you know that?" Will said.

"What do you think? Bobby called me as soon as you left his office," Harry said.

"I understand you knew Miss Spendlove?" Will said.

"That's right," Harry said, whipping out a tube of lip balm, and rapidly running it over his mouth.

"Can I ask how well you knew her, and what you thought of her?" Will asked.

"I barely knew the girl," Harry said. "What did I think of her? I thought she was trouble. Trouble for my client." Harry spoke quickly, as if firing off rounds of ammunition with his sentences.

The lip balm suddenly reappeared, sailed across Harry's mouth, and disappeared again into a pocket. At five feet, six inches tall, with an aggressive manor, Harry Crassman's wiry frame and quick movements gave him an air of barely contained volatility. His high energy and constant motion reminded Will of a Jack Russell terrier. Harry Crassman appeared younger than his seventy-two years, as he darted spryly around the room, never seeming to settle anywhere for more than a few moments. He wore pressed, gray trousers, and a crisp, white shirt with gold cufflinks.

"Trouble in what way?" Will said.

"Trouble in what way, he says!" Harry said. "The girl had trouble written all over her, that's what way!"

Harry puffed out his chest, and approached Will with what could be described an unintended comical version of menace.

"You have to understand something, Detective," he said. "Bobby McCloud is like a son to me. We've been together from the beginning, when the kid was doing dog food commercials, you read me? Back when he was still Rob Hanes. A lot of people want a piece of Bobby," Harry said, "and part of my job is protecting him from unsavory characters. God bless him, but Bobby's not the brightest bulb on the tree, you follow? He doesn't do too well around people who lack good judgment, and there are a lot of creeps out there who are trying to get on the Bobby McCloud gravy train, one way or another."

"So," Harry said, "when it comes to my attention that the dumb schmuck has got himself involved with a girl who peddles *schmattes* and crockpots, an alarm goes off in my head. I think to myself, 'this girl is after a big payday'. You can imagine; I was *schvitzing*! So, naturally, I looked into her background, you understand?"

The lip balm appeared again, streaked across Harry's mouth, and disappeared.

"How did you go about that—looking into her background?" Will asked.

"How did I go about that?" Harry repeated. "What am I? Born yesterday? What else can that mean? I made some calls—contacted a few people—hired a guy to nose around a little."

"I'll need this 'guy's' name," Will said.

"I'll get it from my girl before you leave," Harry said. "Remind me."

"Forgive me, Detective, for speaking like this," Harry said, recovering his indoor voice, "but Fanny was bad news for Bobby. That's all I'm trying to say."

"Did you know about Fanny's gender reassignment surgery?" Will said.

"Yeah," Harry said. "If that information ever got out, it would end Bobby's career in a heartbeat! You think anybody's gonna' pay good money to see a handsome, leading man like Bobby McCloud shtupping his leading lady, once they know his real life girlfriend used to play with his own tinker toy? You follow my meaning?"

"That gives Bobby a pretty strong motive for killing Fanny, wouldn't you say?" Will said.

"Nah, nah," Harry said. "That's not Bobby. He's a pussycat. I mean—yes—it happens to be true that Fanny went nuts when Bobby ended his relationship with her. She went ballistic as a matter of fact, wouldn't take no for an answer. Sent Bobby threatening messages day and night. She even started stalking him outside his office, until she finally gave up. But I'm telling you once and for all, Bobby had nothing to do with this. Definitely not. The kid does not have it in him to do anything like that. I know him better than anybody."

"Were the police contacted about the stalking incident?" Will asked.

"What am I, stupid? An imbecile?" Harry exclaimed. "I can just see it now—a photo of Bobby's production company on the cover of all the tabloids—surrounded by cops—with the headline, 'Bobby McCloud's Stalker Nightmare: Girlfriend Has Secret Schmeckel'. You know how fast these scumbag reporters would uncover Fanny's past? They *live* for crap like that. I couldn't let things go down like that. No way."

More lip balm.

"We decided to lie low, and wait it out," Harry said. "Bobby changed his phone numbers, and we sat tight. Next thing we know, Fanny shows up at a shoot in Queens where Bobby is filming. It was a nightmare—we all had total *schpilkes*! It really shook Bobby up."

"All right, Mr. Crassman," Will said. "Let's say it wasn't Bobby's style. Let's say Bobby is a pussycat."

Harry glared at Will.

"But you're not," Will said. "You're more of a mountain lion, I'd say. Maybe you took it upon yourself to remove the problem? Maybe you 'hired a guy'?"

"Listen to me," Harry said. "Neither Bobby nor myself had anything to do with this unfortunate incident. We will, of course, assist the police in any way we can, and in exchange, I expect not to be harassed or hounded, or treated in any way that might disrupt my business. Same goes for my client. You read me?"

Will regarded Harry calmly, and rose to leave. He paused when he reached the door.

"Thank-you for your time, Mr. Crassman. I'm sorry I can't make you any promises about where the investigation might lead, going forward. So, in the meantime, please don't plan on traveling anywhere in the near future. We'll be in touch."

Chapter 21

*Gluttony is an emotional escape, a sign something is
eating us.*
~ Peter DeVries

Amaleen Stuckey was delighted by the unexpected delivery of a package from GHN. Tearing open the box she found a two pound tin of her favorite confection. A card read:

We hope you enjoyed your recent tour of our studios as much as we enjoyed hosting you. Thank-you for being such a loyal GHN customer. We hope you won't mind, but we took the liberty of checking your purchasing history, and have enclosed a complimentary box of your favorite Mrs. Murchison's Chocolate Covered Pretzel Toffees. Enjoy, and shop often! Your friends at GHN ☺

Flush with a sense of happiness and belonging, Amaleen ripped into the cellophane wrapping, and put two of the buttery-sweet-and-salty candies in her mouth, sighing with pleasure. She wondered if life got any better than this.

***

The police arrived at Amaleen's apartment after being notified that she had failed to show up for work at the Post Office two days in a row, and was not answering her phone. They entered her unit with a key from the landlord.

"Jesus," one of the police officers muttered under her breath when she saw the extent of Amaleen's hoarding. The apartment was virtually impassable. The officer called out but got no response. She and her fellow officer proceeded to make their way cautiously through the cluttered rooms.

They found Amaleen in her bed, deceased. The body looked undisturbed, except for the contorted expression on her face. There were no signs of a break-in or a struggle, and nothing suggested foul play or violence. Amaleen was dressed in a GHN nightgown covered in brightly colored birds. A matching robe lay on the upholstered slipper chair next to the bed that bore the worn sheen of a synthetic fabric. The furnishings were a sorry mixture of cheap and cheerful.

"She's cold," the female officer said.

***

No one had reason to question the family's version of events.

"She had a weak heart," Amaleen's cousin, Augusta, told the Crawford police. "Besides which, her diet wasn't the best—she ate way too many sweets—well, I expect you could judge that for yourself by the look of her. Cousin Honey must have slipped away in her sleep, poor thing. That old heart must've finally just given out."

Connie Biggs, asked permission from the family to dress Amaleen for the viewing. Her choice was obvious. Connie knew exactly what Amaleen's favorite dress was, because they were together when Amaleen purchased it from GHN. They had been at Connie's house eating pizza on a Friday night. The dress was a floral print, and the matching jacket had a ruffled hem, and plastic buttons in the shape of flowers. Amaleen loved it, and Connie had encouraged her to buy it. Everyone at the viewing agreed that Amaleen looked wonderful.

Her death was officially ruled as "natural causes." The citizens of Crawford clucked sympathetically among themselves about the dangers of being overweight, of not getting enough exercise, and eating a poor diet. They commiserated about how sad it would be not having Amaleen to chat with at the post office anymore. A good crowd showed up for her funeral service at Victory in Christ Baptist Church. Dewey Dayton, the manager at the post office, spoke at the service about what a reliable and loyal member of the Crawford Post Office family Amaleen had been. He received a wave of titters from the congregation when he joked about the number of packages that arrived from GHN for her, and how she would always ask to borrow the hand cart to get them all home.

"I reckon nobody knew just exactly what Cousin Honey planned to do with all that stuff," Dewey said, "and I wonder if Cousin Honey even knew, herself. But one thing's for sure, she would have put all those things to good use, because that's the kind of person Cousin Honey was."

This sentiment drew a sympathetic murmur from the crowd, and caused Dewey, himself, to choke up.

"And now," he concluded with a catch in his voice, "now, I guess we'll never know. Rest in peace, Cousin Honey. I know you're up there helping the Good Lord organize his heavenly mail delivery to all the other angels."

Clara Abernathy, sniffling quietly at the organ, broke into a stirring rendition of Amaleen's favorite hymn, *Great Is Thy Faithfulness*.

***

Will popped his head into the Chief's office.

"Got a minute?" he said. Val motioned him in.

"This just came in," he said, handing her a printout. "I think it might be something."

"After we spoke to everybody who was on the GHN tour, I flagged all the names on the list, in case anything else popped up. Something just did. A woman in Crawford, Tennessee, name of Amaleen Stuckey, died unexpectedly yesterday. The cops found her in her apartment after she was reported missing from work."

"Another poisoning?" Val asked.

"Her death was ruled natural, and no autopsy was ordered, because the family said she had a heart condition. She was considerably overweight, so the assumption was that her heart gave out." Will said.

"But, when I spoke to her doctor, he told me that her arrhythmia was non-life threatening, and unlikely to kill her. She was in her early fifties; no alcohol or drug use; no serious health issues; and no domestic violence."

"Where are we going with this?" said the Chief.

"Give me a minute," Will said. "When I interviewed Amaleen a week ago, she mentioned that she was a regular shopper at GHN. I did some digging this morning, and it turns out she had a colorful history there. Besides making weekly purchases from GHN, Fanny Spendlove was something of an obsession with her. GHN had Amaleen flagged in their system because Fanny had received dozens of cards and letters from Amaleen through regular mail, plus hundreds of messages posted on her GHN page and social media."

"Were the messages threatening?" said Val.

"Not specifically threatening, no, but they were *intense*," he replied.

"I was reading up this morning about something called parasocial relationships. It's basically a one-sided relationship, where an individual puts out an obsessive amount of emotional energy toward another person, but this other person isn't even aware of them. It's the kind of thing that's usually directed toward celebrities and sports teams. Amaleen lived in

Tennessee her whole life, and had never—as far as I know—been anywhere near Fanny, so imagine the frame of mind she must have been in when she was about to see Fanny in person at GHN."

"Why would she want to harm Fanny?" Val said. "I'm missing the connection."

"I'm working on that," Will said. "It's possible that in her delusional state of mind something happened to make her snap. I'd like to keep looking into it."

Chapter 22

Pride and grace ne'er dwelt in one place.
~ Scottish proverb

"We'll continue with this stuff on Wednesday," Edwina said to her class, "but in the meantime, as you make your way through Chapter Twelve, please keep in mind that although some of these concepts seem difficult at first, they're what make physics fun, so stick with it, please."

"Now, if you would all close your computers for the few minutes we have left today," she said.

"You have an exam coming up next week, which I realize is making some of you antsy. I'd just like to say something about what it is we're doing in here—to sort of help put things in perspective, if I can."

"In this class—especially for those of you who will go on to do careers in things other than quantum physics—I am essentially trying to teach you how to look at the world around you with a new skill set. A skill set that will allow you to see more clearly what it is you're looking at. If nothing else, your take away from this course should be the general lesson quantum mechanics teaches—that the universe is not what it seems—it's actually much more interesting, once you can see it with all its moving parts. In order to do that, you have to look at things at a level far beyond appearance, if you want to really understand anything. Please get yourselves into the habit of examining things at the deepest level possible; otherwise, you'll miss the boat. And this is not a ride to be missed."

"Okay. See you Wednesday."

***

After class, Edwina rode her bike to the Cushing gym for a yoga class. The airy atmosphere in the yoga studio, with its soft, natural lighting, and restful music playing in the background, was comforting and serene. She unrolled her mat near the front, sat cross-legged, and closed her eyes. The honeyed voice of the instructor lulled her students into a state of relaxation, as she urged them to clear their minds, and focus solely on breathing. Edwina soon began to feel her muscle tension melting away.

During downward doggie pose, there was a muffled commotion near the entrance of the studio. Edwina opened her eyes, and peered from an upside-down vantage point through the 'vee' of her outstretched legs. A latecomer had arrived in class: Rachel Driver. As she made her way to the front of the class, Rachel's muscular build and athletic gait looked comical from Edwina's inverted view, like an oversized bulldog in gym shorts. Edwina knew little about her, other than Rachel was on loan to Cushing's Astronomy & Physics Department from UCLA for the term, she was teaching two graduate level courses at Cushing, and her recent book on condensed matter field theory had been reasonably well-received.

"Hi, neighbor," Rachel whispered, unrolling her mat rather close to Edwina's.

Rude of her not to set up in the back, coming in late like that, Edwina thought. *Plenty of room back there.*

Edwina tried to refocus her attention away from the interloper and back onto her pose, but Rachel's effortful breathing—bordering on grunting—proved distracting. Her feet planted wide apart in a lunging warrior pose—

arms outstretched—Rachel began to wobble. Despite her relatively low center of gravity, she lost her balance, and fell onto her mat with a thud. She was starting to seem like a bull in a china shop.

"You okay?" Edwina said, glancing over.

The instructor made her way quickly over to Rachel's mat. Placing her hands on Rachel's back and shoulder, she helped right the fallen warrior, and re-fashioned her pose into the correct position.

"There you go!" said the instructor. "Perfect warrior."

There was a brief moment after Rachel toppled over when Edwina caught sight of a long scar across her belly—a thin track of fibrous tissue that read like evidence of a Caesarian section. Edwina's interest was piqued, because as far as she knew, Rachel had not arrived at Cushing with any children in tow, so when Rachel asked her out for coffee after class, Edwina agreed to go.

***

Seated across the table from Rachel at Café Mozart, Edwina was able to study her appearance more fully. Rachel's handsome face was free of makeup, and she sported a short hairstyle that complemented the shape of her head. The late afternoon sun highlighted the downy fuzz on her cheeks. On her shirt was the image of an atomic planetary model emblazoned in hot pink across a black background. The caption read, 'Particle Physics Give Me a Hadron'.

"That's some tee shirt," Edwina said affably.

Rachel glanced down, and roared with laughter.

"Isn't it a hoot?" she said. "My ex gave it to me years ago. He used to buy all my clothes for me, as a matter of fact. Now I have to fend for myself. God, I hate shopping. Thank goodness for the home shopping channel!"

"It's not far from here, you know," Edwina said.

"Yeah," Rachel replied. "I actually took my aunt there for a tour. She was so thrilled."

"So, how are you liking Cushing?" Edwina asked.

"Love it," Rachel replied. "Of course, my blood's thinned out from living in southern California for so long, so I'm cold all the time, but I'm getting more acclimated."

"What brings you back east?" Edwina said.

"I have family around here, and I wanted to find a way to spend some time with them. That, and feeling like a change of scenery," Rachel replied.

"How did you like the yoga class?" Edwina said.

"Not sure I'm really built for yoga," Rachel laughed. "My 'happy baby's' a joke! I don't think I'll ever get the hang of it. I should probably stick to cycling."

"Don't be too hard on yourself," Edwina said. "Yoga takes lots of practice. I'm a beginner, too."

Wishing to satisfy her curiosity about Rachel's scar, Edwina thought about how to steer the conversation to Rachel's personal life.

"That must have been great having your ex buy all your clothes for you," she volleyed. "How did you meet him?"

"In college," Rachel replied. I was doing my undergraduate work at U.S.F. He was studying information technology."

"Any children?" Edwina asked.

"Nope," Rachel replied. "He wasn't super keen on that. As a matter of fact, he quit the whole team eventually. Decided he preferred men. Turned out the bum actually had his first man-on-man experience when we were still married, at a conference we attended together. How about that? Right under my nose, and I didn't even realize what was going on."

Edwina wondered why Rachel would lie about having given birth. Had she lost the baby? Had there been an estrangement, and Rachel chose not to speak about having a child she was no longer in touch with? Or was Edwina mistaken altogether about the scar being from a C-section delivery? She decided to leave the subject alone for the time being.

"By some amazing coincidence, I think the guy my ex had the fling with at that conference might actually live in this area," Rachel said. "I think I recognized him the other day in town, by pure chance. What are the odds of that?

"It's funny," she continued, "Maybe it should have been a red flag that my ex-husband liked to do all that shopping for me. I thought he was just being nice, because he knew I hated buying clothes. I never really stopped to consider if there was more to it.

"But speaking of men," Rachel said, "somebody pointed out your boyfriend to me the other day. Cute guy. He's a cop, right?"

"He's a detective," Edwina said, annoyed and offended that Rachel would mention having checked Will out.

"You guys live together, or what?"

Edwina shook her head.

"Any more like him down at the police station? Maybe a friend of his?" Rachel laughed.

"Oh, hey—how about that woman dropping dead at GHN? Is your boyfriend involved in the investigation?"

"Yes," Edwina replied. "He is."

"Wow, no kidding? So, what happened?" Rachel said. "She had kind of a weird name—that woman who died—didn't she? What was it?"

"Fanny Spendlove," Edwina said.

"What a name!" Rachel said. "Sounds like a porn star. How did she die, anyway?"

"Rachel," Edwina said, "I'm sure you can understand—I can't really share information about Will's work. Not that I have all that much to share."

"Oh, heck," Rachel said. "What's wrong with a little inside baseball between colleagues? You must have *some* juicy details about the case?"

"'Fraid not," Edwina said, finishing her coffee.

"Oh, well," Rachel said with a shrug, "no harm, no foul, right? Can't blame a girl for trying."

"You could probably go to Fanny's website on GHN if you're really interested, and find some information," Edwina said.

"Oh, I already tried that, but they don't tell you much of anything," Rachel replied.

The meeting left a funny taste in Edwina's mouth. She wondered why Rachel had invited her out in the first place—was there something Rachel wanted from her? Had she only wanted to know if Edwina could introduce her to one of Will's friends, or was there more to it? Maybe Edwina was imagining things. Maybe Rachel was simply looking for a friend, and if that were the case, Edwina decided she would keep Rachel at arm's length. She was too nosey. Her attempts at immediate intimacy were grating. There was something vaguely predatory about Rachel Driver.

***

"This is Detective Will Tenney with the New Guilford Police in New Hampshire. Who am I speaking to?"

"This is Sgt. Susan Woolery. What can I do for you, Detective Tenney?"

"We think a recent death down there might have some connection to an investigation we're conducting. Can I get the official COD for Amaleen Stuckey?"

"Hang on a second," Sgt. Woolery said.

"It was ruled natural causes, Detective. Ms. Stuckey was found alone in her place of residence."

"Uh-huh," said. Will. "You still investigating?"

"No, there's no activity on it. There were no suspicious circumstances, and the family didn't request any follow-up."

"Can you tell me who found her?" Will asked.

"Hang on a sec," replied the sergeant.

"The deceased's cousin, name of Augusta Shoemaker."

"I wonder if I could get her contact information?" Will said. "And could you send me any other information you have about Miss Stuckey's death?"

"Sure thing, Detective. I'll get it out to you today."

***

"Augusta Shoemaker?" Will said.

"Yes, this is Augusta," the woman said. "Who's calling?"

"My name is William Tenney. I'm a detective with the New Guilford police in New Hampshire. I'm very sorry for the recent loss of your cousin, and I wonder if I might ask you a few questions about her?"

"Cousin Honey? What's this all about? Was she in some kind of trouble?"

"No, no; nothing like that," Will said. "We're investigating a murder up here at the GHN Network on the day your cousin was part of a tour group. We're looking into any possible connections."

"Oh my goodness," Augusta said. "I don't think there could be any connection, Detective. Cousin Honey lived a very quiet life."

How thrilling! Augusta Shoemaker thought. *Wait 'til I tell the girls at bridge tomorrow!*

"Did your cousin have any enemies that you know of? Anyone who might have wished to harm her?"

"Oh, no," Augusta said. "Everyone liked Cousin Honey. She worked at the post office, you know. She was very popular. Just about the whole town came to her funeral."

"Was she looking forward to the trip to GHN, if you know? Did she discuss it with you at all?" Will asked. "Did she tell you anything about it when she got back to Crawford?"

"You should probably speak to Connie Biggs," Augusta replied. "Connie was Cousin Honey's best friend. That's who she went up there with. I talked to Cousin Honey right before she left, but she was in one of her moods. Seemed like she had something bothering her. She was always a very moody girl, ever since we were kids."

"Do you know what?"

"I'm sorry to say that Cousin Honey didn't confide very much in me," Augusta said.

"Do you know if your cousin was seeing anyone? A boyfriend, maybe?"

"Oh, no," Augusta said. "She didn't have any interest in that kind of thing. She was a little bit of an odd duck, Detective. She had her job at the post office, her friend, Connie, and her GHN, and that was about it. She was a sweet, simple soul, God rest her."

***

"Miss Biggs, this is William Tenney from the New Guilford Police in New Hampshire. We spoke on the phone recently. I'm very sorry for the loss of your friend, Amaleen Stuckey. Would it be all right if I asked you a few questions about her?"

"I can't even believe she's gone," Connie Biggs said, her voice catching. "I just can't believe it."

"I understand, ma'am," Will said. "Would you mind talking to me for just a few minutes? I'm sorry to trouble you, but it's important."

"What's all this about?" she said, sniffling.

"An employee at GHN died at the studio the day you and Amaleen were on the tour."

"Oh, my," Connie said. "I'm sorry to hear that. What does this have to do with me and Cousin Honey, though?"

"The person who died was Fanny Spendlove, and I understand Amaleen was a particular fan of hers. I thought you might be able to help me out with our investigation," Will said.

"Fanny Spendlove, dead? Gosh, that's awful. She was Cousin Honey's favorite. We got to see her do a live show the day we were there. It was so exciting," Connie said. "What happened?"

"She was poisoned," Will said.

"Poisoned! Oh, my goodness, that's dreadful," Connie said. "Poor Fanny."

"Was Amaleen upset about anything in particular around the time of your trip? Did she seem preoccupied? Anything you might be able to remember—any little thing at all—could be very helpful."

"I don't understand, Detective," Connie said. "What does our trip have to do with Fanny's death?"

"Probably nothing, ma'am," Will said. "We just have to be very thorough with our reports. So, can you think of anything Amaleen was concerned or worried about, having to do with your trip?"

"Hm, well, I do remember when I first told her I'd won the contest, and that I was taking her with me, I expected her to be super excited and happy, but she wasn't. I asked her why, but she wouldn't tell me. But as the trip got closer, she got in a better mood about it, and started to get excited, almost like she couldn't wait to get there."

"Did you ever find out what was bothering her? Did she say anything specific you can remember?" Will said.

"Not really. That was just how Cousin Honey was," Connie replied. "She was moody like that, and you just had to roll with it."

Chapter 23

There is only one happiness in this life, to love and be loved.
~ George Sand

Will pulled onto Canaan Farm Road late at night under a black sky decorated with moonlit clouds. Edwina ran downstairs when she heard him turn into the driveway.

"Brought you something," he said, dropping an issue of *People* magazine with Bobby McCloud on the cover on the kitchen table. "Thought you might be interested in reading up about him."

"How did it go?" she said. "Tell me everything."

"Got anything to eat?" he said. "I didn't have a chance to get dinner."

***

Will bit into the grilled cheese and avocado sandwich Edwina made, and, at her urging, began a faithful narrative of the day's events that included an impression of Harry Crassman's repeated applications of lip balm as he paced around his office. She poured two glasses of wine as she listened to Will's description of Bobby McCloud's sumptuous offices in a gated mews near Washington Square; and Harry Crassman's agency, and his bombast; and all the rest of it.

"Do you think Bobby McCloud really goes scuba diving with his dog?" she said.

"Apparently so," Will said.

"Think he's involved with Fanny's death?"

"Maybe," Will replied. "He knows all about aquariums, and he knows about cone snails, because of all the time he's spent in Australia. And he's got excellent motive."

"What was your overall sense of him?" Edwina asked. "You know, I mean as an *actual* murderer. Think he's capable of it?"

"I think everybody is, given the right set of circumstances. But, between the two of them, I think it's more likely that Harry Crassman is involved," Will said. "That would follow the pattern of their relationship. Harry's the tough guy/father figure. He takes care of things, looks after Bobby, runs interference for him. He's extremely protective of Bobby. I don't think there's much Harry wouldn't do for him."

"Including kill somebody?"

"Or, *have* them killed," Will said.

"What about Fanny's colleagues at the network? You said a few of them have gripes against her. How are they stacking up as suspects?" Edwina said.

"What about Harry's ex-wife, for example?" she said. "Maybe she and Harry were in it together? She would certainly have opportunity. Maybe Harry even paid her to put the snail in the tank."

"I wouldn't put it past her," Will said.

"Maybe Esther didn't even know the snail was poisonous, and she agreed to do it as a prank," Edwina said. "Then, after the fact, Harry'd be able to say Esther did the deed all on her own, and that he had nothing to do with it."

"That works all right on paper," Will said, "but I don't see Harry and Esther teaming up. There's too much bitterness between those two for a partnership."

"Think they could just be putting on a show for you, pretending to hate each other's guts, and secretly be in cahoots?" Edwina said.

"Possible, I suppose," he said.

Edwina was sleepy from the late hour, the wine, and the warmth from the stove, but her curiosity trumped the desire for sleep. Bedtime could wait.

"What about that other guy from GHN—what's his name?" she yawned.

"Brad Pilfer?"

"What about him and the woman he was having an affair with?" she said.

"Yeah, they both have motive, and the lack of moral compass to act on it," Will said. "Fanny was blackmailing Brad Pilfer. When she and Pilfer worked at an investment firm in New York, Pilfer got caught for embezzling. The firm never pressed charges, but Fanny knew about it, and used it against Pilfer to get the job at GHN. Plus some extra cash on the side."

"And Mary Lou?" Edwina said.

"Fanny was her number one rival at the network. Mary Lou would've been only too happy to have her out of the way. Still, it's a long way from proving anything," Will said.

"There's definitely no shortage of suspects in this thing, but the murder weapon still makes no sense to me," he said. Why choose such an odd and risky way to kill someone? Why go to all that trouble? How did the killer even know Fanny would pick the snail up, and that it would bite her? It seems like a lot to leave to chance. There's something else going on with this cone snail thing. Something. I'm not seeing."

Edwina's eyelids were starting to droop.

"What do you say we turn in?" Will said, carrying his plate to the sink. "We can talk more tomorrow. Come on, sleepyhead."

Chapter 24

Advertising is the rattling of a stick inside a swill bucket.
~ George Orwell

Sheldon Woodsmall—aka Chef Gordo—was GHN's in-house culinary guru, an idol to tens of thousands of home cooks around the country who eagerly tried out his every new recipe, collected his cookbooks, and purchased his signature kitchenware products. With his outsized presence (Chef Gordo clocked in at six feet four inches tall; two hundred and twenty-five pounds), and a personality to match, GHN fans loved his good-natured, avuncular persona. Chef Gordo's booming voice had a curious, prerecorded quality, almost robotic, as if every single word were scripted. To the delight of his followers, his shows were peppered with quaint, southern expressions ('folks, you gotta' run with the big dogs or stay on the porch!'), and he wore aprons from his own, personal collection on the air, that said things like, *Good Lookin' is doin' the cookin'!* or *Caution! Extremely Hot!* Many of these aprons had been sent in by his fans, who regularly posted their undying loyalty to him and his scrumptious, butter-laden recipes. His segments accounted for a lion's share of GHN's revenue.

Chef Gordo's success at the network afforded him the leverage to make certain demands—among them, time off whenever he wanted it. In fact, he was such a prima donna, the Board of Directors reviewed his contract every time it came up for renewal with an eye to cutting him loose, and replacing him, but his shows continued to bring in too much money for the network to justify his firing. The staff had gotten used to Chef Gordo's rants and shrill demands. During his frequent time off, other hosts were asked to fill in for him. Ratings tended to drop when Chef Gordo was away, but not disastrously.

Mary Lou Flowers was tapped to host one of Gordo's shows when he decided at the last minute he needed to get away to the Greek islands for a few days. Certain aspects of this arrangement caused deep resentment in Mary Lou. Most of all, it was the fact that absolutely nothing about cooking interested her. Kitchens—and everything in them, with the exception of liquor cabinets and ice-makers—bored her senseless. She didn't know a pressure cooker from a bread maker, and didn't care. 'Freezer to table' was Mary Lou's battle cry in the kitchen. She was a microwave maven through and through.

Cooking demonstrations were important aspects of Chef Gordo's shows, and since Mary Lou didn't feel remotely at home in the kitchen, she worried that these segments would cast her in a clumsy light. These demonstrations invariably involved sampling quantities of fattening foods (homemade ice cream makers outsold juicers ten to one), and Mary Lou was not one to shy away from eating. After all, zealous endorsements from hosts in the form of gasped delights and other such exclamations boosted sales tremendously. Customers weren't necessarily willing to spend $38.40 a month for automatic deliveries of Aunt Pauline's coffee cakes—a different flavor each month--without seeing proof with their own eyes of how scrumptious the cakes were. Accordingly, Mary Lou did her best to push sales by swooning with pleasure, and rolling her eyes in appreciation each time she shoveled a forkful of the cake into her mouth. Hosting these shows meant gaining weight, and Mary Lou blamed Chef Gordo, in part, for her ballooning dress size. Determined to salvage something useful from her fattening servitude, Mary Lou decided she would go on a fishing expedition with Walter Babcock, to see if she could glean any information about the investigation. Walter was privy to gossip from the warehouse, the boom operators, gaffers, grips, and fellow cameramen.

"Hey, Walt," she called to him a few minutes before "Effortless Cooking with Chef Gordo" was about to start. "When do you get off today?"

"Right after this show," Walter Babcock said.

"Want to stick around and have a bite?"

"I think that can be arranged," Walter replied, cheerfully patting his ample belly.

As host of the show that day, Mary Lou welcomed the inventor of a non-stick, self-cleaning crepe-making appliance, who demonstrated his creation by preparing Crepes Benedict, broccoli-cheddar crepes, and six other crepe concoctions. Each time Mary Lou faked a food climax, sales spiked. The final crepe recipe was "chocolate death", which involved heavy cream, butter, sugar, chocolate, and marshmallows. She felt queasy after one bite, and hoped she could hold it together for the remainder of the broadcast.

The second part of the show featured a deluxe air fryer, at a special, introductory offer price. Despite protestations from her stomach, Mary Lou managed to enact more food rapture, exuding delight as her guest whipped up batches of onion rings, chicken wings, and French fries, all the while feeling her waistline expand in real time on camera. While sales went through the roof, she ran a mental tally of the number of calories she would have to work off the next day at the gym.

When the segment finally, blessedly ended, Mary Lou motioned Walter Babcock onto the set, where he tucked into a platter of chicken wings, French fries, and crepes. Mary Lou gnawed on three antacid tablets.

"Heard anything new about Fanny's murder?" she said.

Walter looked up through a mouthful of fries.

"One of the guys was telling me the police took Fanny's notes from her last show," he said. "I guess they're hoping there might be some kind of useful information in them."

"Oh, really?" Mary Lou said, stifling a burp. "Like what, I wonder?"

"Beats me," Walter said.

"So, no word about the police having any suspects, yet?" Mary Lou said, pushing a plate of deep fried pickles toward him.

"Not that I know of," he shrugged. "I just can't figure out how a poisonous snail could get into that tank. It's so weird. Kind of gives me the creeps. I was talking to some of the guys in the warehouse about it, and they said nobody down there even saw the aquarium. They said it was delivered directly from the manufacturer to Fanny's set."

"I wonder if the police are questioning anybody besides GHN personnel?" she said.

"I heard there might be somebody at the college they're looking at. Could you pass those?" Walter said, pointing to the onion rings.

"So, Walt, what about you? Got any theories of your own?" she said.

"Well," he said, "I hate to say it, but I don't think too many folks around here liked Fanny all that much. Seems like people aren't too broken up about it."

"Got anyone in particular in mind?" she asked.

"Not really," he replied. "You?"

"I can't imagine who'd want to hurt Fanny," Mary Lou said.

Chapter 25

We forge the chains we wear in life.
~ Charles Dickens

"Put her through—if you must," Harry Crassman said, holding the line.

"Harry?"

"What is it this time, Esther?"

"Just wanted to say hello to my least favorite person," his ex-wife chirped, "and to let you know I'm following the Fanny Spendlove case with keen interest. So shocking how it happened right under my own nose. But I guess you know all about it."

"I'm busy, Esther, what do you want?" Harry said.

"Just thinking about you and Wonder Boy....wondering if the two of you might be involved, in some way? I know how much the two of you stand to lose if certain facts get out," Esther said. "You must be worried sick, you poor schmuck—I hope that ulcer's not acting up."

"Bobby and I aren't the only ones who stand to lose," Harry said. "Did you forget you're on the same gravy train, you dumb mutt? How do you think I manage to pay your alimony every month? Maybe *you're* the one who's involved? What'd you do—put poison in her lipstick?"

"Now, why would I do that?" Esther replied.

"Anything to spite me, right?" Harry said. "Anyway, you don't know what you're talking about. As usual.

And even if you did know what you were talking about, you still wouldn't know anything, you stupid bitch."

"Okay, Harry, whatever you say," Esther replied breezily. "But I hear on the grapevine that the tabloids are sniffing around for information about Fanny, and I have to wonder how much they'd be willing to pay for certain information about her past, and about her love life?"

Harry stared down at the busy avenue. The world seemed to be sailing along as normal, oblivious and uncaring about the fact that his gilded kingdom was under siege. Not one fellow human looked up from the teeming sidewalk below to give Harry a sympathetic glance or a reassuring thumbs-up. What was the world coming to, when he could feel so desolate and isolated despite the great rumble of humanity right outside his window?

Harry spoke wearily, a sudden headache causing a sharp pain in his left eyeball.

"How much this time?" he said.

Chapter 26

*There are strings in the human heart that had better not
be vibrated.*
~ Charles Dickens

Bobby had read the email countless times since first receiving it, still hardly knowing what to make of it. Since living in the public eye, he had steeled himself for such a possibility, knowing that his fame might attract shadows from the past—especially after the recent magazine interview in *People.* He had never particularly cared or wondered who his birth parents were. His adopted parents had been nothing but supportive and kind, and Bobby was content to think of them as his only parents. Now, after a lifetime, someone who might be his biological mother was reaching out to him through the electronic ether.

Your father left before I knew I was pregnant, the email said, *and I never told him about you. Neither of us—as young as we were, and with careers to pursue— was in a position to raise a child. If you choose not see me, I will, of course, understand.*

Regardless of whether or not we meet, please know that I wish you the very best in life, and I am overjoyed to know your childhood was a happy one, assuming the article about you in People Magazine *is accurate.*

Bobby thought for days about a response—or if he would even give one. He had no wish to meet the woman. It was too little, too late, and besides that, he had every reason to suspect her motives. He was, after all, a high profile celebrity. When he finally did answer her, the tone of his reply was crafted carefully with cordial formality, like lines from a script. He made it clear he did not wish to meet her under any circumstances, but that he wished her well. She replied that she was naturally disappointed, but understood completely, and once again, wished him all the best. The letter had asked nothing of him except a chance to meet. Bobby had little, if any, ambivalence about refusing her request, except for the idlest curiosity about her—what she looked like, what she sounded like—and this lingered at the edge of his mind for a few weeks.

Searching online for anything new in the Fanny Spendlove investigation, he came up empty handed. There was no fresh information to be had, only a handful of brief newspaper items that repeated the same, basic facts. The investigation seemed to be going nowhere, and he now wondered if he should make the police aware of the email from this woman who claimed to be his biological mother. He wouldn't want to be accused of withholding evidence, just in case it turned out the woman was somehow involved.

Bobby reached into the desk drawer, and rifled around until he found what he was looking for. He wove the card back and forth through his fingers, and stared at it, as if waiting for it to give him a signal.

New Guilford Police Department
Grafton County
Detective Wm. Tenney

Chapter 27

The streets were dark with something more than night.
~ Raymond Chandler

Will sat at his desk surrounded by case files. He opened the issue of *People* with Bobby McCloud on the cover, and reread the article.

Given up for adoption by a single mother, Bobby had been raised by Janice and Robert Hanes, with whom he enjoyed an idyllic sounding childhood in the Midwest. Will studied the photos of Bobby as a boy, dressed in a cowboy outfit standing next to a new bicycle with a bow tied on the handlebars—wading in a pond up to his knees with a fishing pole—blowing out candles on a birthday cake. He looked happy. The piece described how, as a teenager, Bobby had left for New York after getting hooked on acting in high school. Harry Crassman had discovered him at the age of nineteen in a dog food commercial, and signed him on as a client. So the story went.

Will revisited the idea of Esther Rubenstein being a third musketeer in a nefarious alliance with Bobby and Harry. Esther's dislike of Fanny, bolstered by the threat to her financial well-being if Harry were to lose his star client, was sufficient motive. It was a strong likelihood that Harry would no longer be able to afford Esther's inflated alimony payments if the paying public found out about Bobby's affair with a transgender woman. Bobby's star was sure to fall in such a scenario.

Will figured Esther must have known about Fanny's sexual reassignment surgery because of the close, physical proximity in which they worked together. Esther was good at collecting information, and she wielded it like a weapon when she wanted. She seemed to know everyone's peccadilloes. Did her knowledge of Fanny's secrets put her at the center of the investigation?

Esther's reasons for disliking Fanny were many. The feelings Esther held dear about classic beauty and glamour, forged by her past in the New York theater were routinely derided and demeaned by Fanny. Not only did Fanny not know who any of the iconic actresses in Esther's photos were, neither did she care. Will knew Fanny's crass self-centeredness was galling to Esther. Esther bitterly resented the fact that Fanny openly thumbed her nose at everything Esther valued. Cause enough to stir murderous feelings. Had Esther felt the need to remove Fanny for being such an unapologetic philistine, as well as being a financial threat to her alimony payments from Harry?

On the other hand, would Esther really be willing to risk losing the security of the established and comfortable life she had? Would she be willing to abet her ex-husband, whom she loathed, in a scheme to kill Fanny? Certainly Harry, who stood to lose his livelihood if Bobby's career tanked, had a volatile temper. Perhaps he had acted alone, without the aid of his ex-wife. Perhaps he had 'called a guy' who took care of things. Harry was plenty resourceful. He was, after all, the brains behind the Bobby McCloud brand.

And what about Bobby, himself? Bobby followed Harry's every directive, it seemed, and Will could just about imagine Bobby being persuaded into taking part in such a plot. Harry and his star client had the most to lose. Harry was convinced that Bobby's career would be over in an instant if it his relationship with Fanny got out, and since Bobby was Harry's only A-list client, if Bobby's career went south, both their incomes would tank. It would be dog commercials again for Bobby, and Harry would be left scrounging for B-list projects. *Gornisht.*

Something caught Will's eye as he started to close the magazine. It was a caption under one of the photos––a photo of Bobby at his production company office, the same office where Will had interviewed him.

"I never had any interest in searching for my birth parents, even though friends have often encouraged me to."

What if a member of Bobby's birth family had decided to contact Bobby after seeing the article? Will had interviewed and ruled out members of Bobby's adoptive family, including Mr. and Mrs. Hanes, a handful of nieces and nephews, cousins, and aunts and uncles, but no one from Bobby's birth family.

Could an opportunistic birth parent—or half sibling––be in the picture? Could someone from Bobby's biological family have uncovered Bobby's dalliance with Fanny, and found out about her past as Gus Prestopino, and tried to exploit the situation to their advantage? Bobby had mentioned to Will that Fanny put up pictures of Bobby on her GHN page, but Harry made her take them down. Had somebody seen them, and dug deeper into Fanny's past? Had someone even concocted a scheme to frame Bobby for Fanny's murder? If Bobby ended up in prison, a birth relation could lay claim to Bobby's fortune.

Too many ifs, thought Will. *I'm drifting too far afield.*

Dipping back into the files, he reviewed the notes from his interviews with Mary Lou Flowers and Brad Pilfer. Pilfer had been paying Fanny money to buy her silence about his embezzlement from their prior employer, McAndrews Larsen. Currently, Pilfer earned a comfortable salary as vice president of marketing and sales at GHN. If the real reason for leaving his old firm ever came out, GHN would let him go, and he could run the risk, at his age, of being unemployable. And with a huge mortgage to pay, and a taste for expensive cars and family vacations, Brad Pilfer had every reason to want Fanny out of the picture.

Lots of motives to go around, it seemed.

Then there was Mary Lou Flowers, a woman scorned. Edged out of the top dog position at the network by the ambitious, younger Fanny, and shamed by her bosses for her weight gain and her drinking, Mary Lou could hear the clock ticking on her career. She had become fixated on Fanny as the source of all her problems. As a criminal duo, Brad Pilfer and Mary Lou Flowers might be capable of anything. They had in common all the moral fiber of a jellyfish.

**

Edwina could not get to sleep. She tried not to disturb Will as she extricated herself from the blankets, pulled on a pair of socks, and padded downstairs to the kitchen. Enfolding herself in a lap blanket, she nestled into the rocking chair, and gazed out the windows at the faintly outlined trees in the darkness. She closed her eyes, and drowsily let the shadowy tableau of woods morph into a swirling field of energy, made up of billions of subatomic particles, merrily vibrating. Soon she drifted off to sleep.

Two hours later, she woke with a start, and after a moment's disorientation, she ran upstairs.

"Will!" she whispered. The clock said 4:42 a.m.

"Will?"

"Mm?" he muttered.

"Sorry to wake you, but I have to talk to you."

Will rubbed his eyes, blinked a few times, and slowly sat up.

"I think I might have figured something out," she said. "Remember when I told you how strange it was that Don Gaylord asked me about my lunch with Phil Kimby as soon as I got back from Boston? The more I thought about it, it didn't make sense, because as far as I was aware, Don Gaylord and Phil Kimby know each other, but I didn't think they kept in close touch, so how did Don know I had lunch with Phil? Had Don and Phil been in recent touch? And if so, why?"

"Then I was thinking about how Don reacted when he heard that Phil Kimby asked me to join the Quantum Project at the NSA. Paolo thinks maybe Don knew about Phil being head of the project down there, and that Don was angling to be invited on board at The Agency.

"I think as soon as Don heard that Phil had contacted me, he probably got in touch with Phil, and tried to pump him for information about the project. Phil must have mentioned he and I were meeting in Boston over the conference weekend, and Don assumed I had signed on with Phil's NSA team."

"Why would all of that matter so much to Don?" Will said.

"I'm not exactly sure—he's just compulsive. No question Don has a brilliant mind," Edwina said, "but he's not the most stable element on the chart. He can be a tad paranoid, and he likes to keep tabs on everyone— on their successes and failures and job promotions, and book reviews, and their personal lives—anything and everything he can dig up. Phil is aware of all that, and would never involve Don with national security."

"So, where does all that get us?" Will said.

"For one thing," Edwina said, "it might help make sense of why Don and Jimmy have been having trouble.

I'll bet you anything that Don lobbied Phil for a spot on the NSA team, and he was rejected. Don can be very vindictive, you know. You should've heard him going on and on about getting bumped from some radio interview. It made him absolutely nuts—he was swearing vengeance!"

"What's the connection with Jimmy?" Will said.

"Maybe Don's been in a rage ever since he was rejected for the NSA project, and it all came out against Jimmy."

"Hm. If Gaylord was in touch with Phil Kimby, that would explain how he knew you and Phil were getting together in Boston," Will said.

"Exactly!" Edwina said.

"I'll talk to Val tomorrow," Will said. "Then I'll get in touch with Phil Kimby, and find out whether or not he's been in recent communication with Gaylord."

Daybreak was readying itself for show time. As night eased itself toward dawn, sepia-colored light crept into the room, and the sun began its slow emergence. Birds chirped on cue.

"Want to get up, or try to get some more sleep?" she said.

Will stretched.

"Might as well get up," he said, "and get an early start. Lots to do."

***

Edwina sat at the table with a mug of tea, a bowl of oatmeal, and a book about 18th C. German astronomer, Caroline Herschel, propped up against the teapot. Will was having scrambled eggs as he read the news. This tableau of genteel domesticity was interrupted when a call came in on Will's phone.

"Will Tenney," he said, getting up from the table, and heading for the back door.

"Yes, of course; now is fine, if you like," he said, stepping outside.

Edwina watched him through the window for the duration of the call, and observed that whoever was on the other end did most of the talking.

When Will returned inside, Edwina regarded him intently. She refilled his cup from the teapot.

"Anything interesting?" she said.

"That," Will said, "was Bobby McCloud. Looks like we have a development. It seems that his birth mother– –or someone claiming to be—got in touch with him recently, out of the clear blue. He wouldn't tell me the woman's name, but he thought she might be relevant to the investigation. He didn't say how, and I don't think he has anything specific in mind—other than the timing struck him as odd."

"Why wouldn't he tell you her name?" Edwina said.

"He said she doesn't want the publicity. She doesn't want all the sudden attention of being Bobby McCloud's mother."

"It does seem curious that she would get in touch with him now, in the middle of the investigation," Edwina said.

"The explanation for that could be the recent article in *People* magazine. She told him that's how she found out Bobby was the son she gave up for adoption," Will said. "Before that, she had no idea of what became of him. Don't forget; he changed his name from Hanes to McCloud when he became an actor, so the birth mother had lost track of him."

"Do you think it could be about money?" Edwina said. "This woman finds out that the biological son she put up for adoption years ago is a wealthy celebrity— maybe she's looking for a handout?"

"I asked Bobby about that," Will said, "and he emphatically denied it. He says the reason she got in touch was just for a chance to meet him. Which he declined to do."

"Why?" Edwina said. "Did he say?"

"He said he preferred to let sleeping dogs lie," Will said.

"How mysterious. Why do you think Bobby called you?" Edwina said.

"He kind of hedged around that," Will said. "What he did say is that he thought I should know this woman was 'in the picture'. Reading between the lines, I'd say he was rattled by hearing from her, and that he thinks she might have something to do with Fanny's death....but he was doing everything in his power to keep from admitting that to me. And maybe even to himself."

Chapter 28

Einstein, in the special theory of relativity, proved that different observers in different states of motion, see different realities.
~ Leonard Susskind

Edwina paid little attention to the rumbling noises coming from her stomach, preferring to concentrate on the mathematical expression written on the blackboard, which she had been tinkering with for the past hour.

After an additional thirty minutes, she began to feel light-headed from hunger. Setting the chalk aside, she scrabbled around under a pile of books and papers on the desk, and soon emerged with a plastic bag containing a sandwich.

Holding the sandwich in one hand, she flipped the blackboard to its blank side. On it she wrote:

Fanny Spendlove

Suspects + Motives

Mary Lou Flowers—jealousy + resentment over Fanny's success at GHN

Brad Pilfer—Fanny was blackmailing him

Esther, makeup woman—1) Afraid of losing alimony payments from Harry C if Fanny's past came out (ruining Bobby McCloud's career) 2) general hatred of Fanny

Bobby McCloud (ex-boyfriend)—Needed to protect his image + career

Harry Crassman, Bobby's agent—same as above

Bobby's birthmother?—$$$?

Edwina searched her mind for other dots that might help fill in this sketchy picture. Were there additional forces at work? For instance, was it happenstance that the timing of Rachel Driver's appearance in New Guilford coincided with Fanny's murder? Rachel was, after all, familiar with GHN; she shopped there. That was a connection of sorts, albeit tenuous. Rachel had even said she'd visited the GHN studio, hadn't she?

Was there more to Rachel being in New Guilford than met the eye? Rachel had mentioned to Edwina that she saw the man her ex-husband had had the affair with—spotted him in New Guilford, allegedly, to Rachel's great surprise. Edwina wondered if maybe Rachel already knew the man was in New Guilford, and if so, was she stalking him? Was she at Cushing this semester in order to settle an old score? What if Rachel's ex-husband was still involved with this man? If so, then her ex was living in the area, too, and maybe Rachel had come to New Guilford to exact some sort of revenge against both of them? Edwina needed to find out more about Rachel's ex.

Sitting down at the desk, Edwina recalled Rachel saying that her husband's affair had taken place during a conference, which could mean her ex most likely worked in a related field to Rachel's. Oh, that's right, Edwina remembered; Rachel said her husband had studied information technology. It shouldn't be too difficult to figure out which conference it had been. She looked up conferences relating to mathematics, astrophysics, info tech, and the like, that had taken place during the years Rachel would have been in graduate school, in or near the San Francisco area.

She soon zeroed in on a symposium at the Embarcadero Center, called, 'Information Systems in the Quantum Age', on a date that fit the timeline. She scrolled through the site, studying the lists of speakers, invited guests, panelists, and attendees, and looking for photographs. The scholarly community was not a huge one, and it was possible Edwina knew someone who had been there, whom she would plan to contact, and find out if they knew Rachel or her then-husband. There might've even been someone at that particular conference who was currently teaching at Cushing, or somewhere in the area. If so, she would attempt to glean some useful information from them. It was a tedious task, and it paid off in spades. Listed in attendance at the Symposium was none other than,

Dr. Donald Gaylord, Ph.D., Cushing College

Had Donald crossed paths with Rachel and her ex-husband at the conference? Did Donald know Rachel from before she arrived at Cushing? He certainly didn't seem to like Rachel much—what had he called her—a truck driver? Yes, Donald had been quite disparaging about Rachel Driver. Dots were starting to collide, and Edwina knew there would be nothing random about the picture those dots formed, once she could make it out. Paths had crossed, and she just had to make sense of the trajectories. Forces at work result from interactions. Newton's Third Law of Motion told her so.

Edwina sat back in the chair, and closed her eyes, absorbed in this new line of thought. She wondered if Donald might even be the Mr. X with whom Rachel's ex-husband had had the dalliance? Donald undoubtedly had a reputation as a charmer. A string of students—male and female—had developed unrequited crushes on him over the years, and it was well known around the Department that Donald used his powers of seduction to encourage this sort of hero worship. It was no stretch of the imagination to think that he had enticed Mr. Rachel Driver into a relationship during that conference years earlier. Had this affair been the wedge that destroyed Rachel's marriage? With nothing more to unearth from the symposium site, Edwina typed in a new search: California marriage records.

It was not long before Edwina let out a little yelp of discovery. She sat stunned, staring at the screen. When she finally got up from the desk to go to the blackboard, she wrote:

Rachel Driver and Gus Prestopino (aka Fanny Spendlove) were once husband and wife.

It all seemed to be fitting together. Rachel had said that by the time she and Gus parted ways, his romantic interests had shifted to men. Did Rachel know more than she was letting on? Did she know her ex-husband had become Fanny Spendlove, darling of the home shopping network? Was Rachel's jocular, breezy manner a cover? Was she actually at Cushing on a deadly mission? When Rachel mentioned to Edwina at coffee about wanting to spend time with her family in the east, was the 'family' she was referring to Fanny Spendlove? Edwina stared at the blackboard, and contemplated the calculus of Rachel Driver as a murderer. Perhaps Rachel had some sort of breakdown when she learned her ex had transitioned to Fanny Spendlove?

Edwina wrote Rachel's name on the board.

With the adrenaline of discovery rushing in her ears, she grabbed her phone, and punched out: *You coming over tonight?*

***

"But, what would motivate her *now*?" Will said, bending down to slide a roasting pan into the oven. In her excited state, Edwina was standing so close to him that he backed into her when he stepped away from the oven.

"Sorry," she said.

"Why now?" Edwina said. "I think I figured that out. "Let's say Rachel lost track of Gus, and didn't know anything about the sexual reassignment surgery—until very recently. After all, there was no reason for them to stay in touch after they divorced—there were no kids, or anything.

"When I had coffee with her, Rachel mentioned GHN," Edwina said, standing by Will's elbow as he rinsed vegetables. "She said her husband—Gus, that is—used to buy all her clothes for her, and that after they split up, she had to start shopping for herself. But, since she hates shopping, buying clothes online was the perfect solution. So, we know Rachel was a GHN viewer. I think she must have recognized Fanny as her ex-husband, Gus. And when she did, she flipped out."

"As long as you're tailing me," Will remarked, "want to peel and chop those parsnips?"

"So, once Rachel recognized Fanny as Gus," she said, running a peeler over the parsnips, "she got the job teaching at Cushing, so she could see Fanny in person, and confront her, or something. Fanny must have agreed to meet with Rachel, and then something happened that made the meeting go really badly, and Rachel decided to kill Fanny."

"Over what, though?" Will said. "What could make their meeting go so far off the tracks? I'm not sure I buy the revenge thing—that Rachel felt so humiliated or angry about Gus's transformation that she murdered him for it. There has to be more motive than that to seriously consider Rachel as a murder suspect."

Edwina chopped the vegetables as she thought this over. Will was right; the connection Edwina had uncovered about Rachel being married to Gus wasn't enough to point to Rachel as the murderer.

"You said there were no kids from their marriage, right?" Will said.

Edwina nearly lopped off her thumb as she cut into the fat end of a parsnip. She set the knife down on the cutting board, and turned to face Will.

"Yeah, I did say that," she said, "didn't I? But, you know something? Now I'm not so sure. Remember that day Rachel practically stalked me to my yoga class? I happened to get a glimpse of a scar on her belly, and I thought it looked an awful lot like a scar from a C-section. But, when I asked her later at coffee if she had any children, she said 'no'.

"But," Edwina said, "what if she and Gus *did* have a baby together? The child would be in his or her twenties or so, now. Maybe that's what brought Rachel back east—something to do with the child she had with Gus Prestopino. Maybe that's what she needed to talk to Fanny about—some kind of crisis with their child, maybe a health crisis—and Rachel needed Fanny's help. And, what if Fanny completely refused to acknowledge the child, or the situation, or anything, and turned her back on the whole thing? Now, there's motive for you."

"Okay," Will said. "For the moment, let's say that's exactly what happened. Rachel has a child whom Gus Prestopino fathered, and that child is now in need of a kidney transplant, or money, or some kind of help. Fanny turns her back on Rachel's request for help, and Rachel kills Fanny in anger. Why would Rachel choose such a bizarre way to kill her? Such a risky, crazy method like cone snail poisoning, when there are much easier, more reliable ways to go about it? Doesn't make sense."

Edwina was still flush with excitement from discovering the connection between Rachel and Gus/Fanny, and was trying not to let Will's reasoning dampen her enthusiasm. Even so, she knew she was trying to force a picture into place that wasn't ready to take shape. Why on earth *would* Rachel put a poisonous snail in Fanny's tank? The idea was crazy.

Edwina was accustomed to difficult, time-consuming proofs; it was the arduous nature of her work. She anticipated that new facts would come to light in the coming days. She just needed to wait it out. Solutions to the most interesting problems required the most patience and fortitude. In the meantime, she would just keep thinking.

***

Edwina was the first to admit that good ideas sometimes came to her in dreams. Sleep state was the time thoughts and ideas were completely free from editing—free to roam around, to mingle, and to mate with other thoughts and ideas, and produce new ones that might never have taken shape during waking hours.

When she awoke the following morning it was from a night of such dreams. She bided her time before sharing her new ideas with Will, so that she could get her thoughts organized. She didn't want to blurt out a disjointed narrative that might sound half-baked. She wanted to make sure whatever she had to tell him would hold up in the clear light of day.

Will sat across the table eating scrambled eggs, and reading.

"Will," she said. "I think I might've figured something out, although I'm not positive, of course. It's going to sound nuts, but it's not. It's actually not nuts at all."

"I'm all ears," he said, looking up.

"Okay, here goes. Let's say Rachel Driver and Gus Prestopino had that baby. Like you said, if they did, they probably would have given the child up for adoption. Years go by, and the child grows up. They don't know what became of the baby after the adoption. Gus may not even know a baby existed.

"Now," she said, "there are a few lines in your investigation that look like they run on parallel tracks, as if there's no connection between them, but I think they actually intersect. Think of the moons of a planet, or the planets around the sun—all orbiting around the same center, held in place by the same thing: gravity. It doesn't look like they're connected, but they are. They're all bound together by the same force.

"We've got one storyline where Rachel and Gus have a baby, give it up for adoption at birth, and have no idea what becomes of that child when he or she grows up. Second, we've got the story of Bobby McCloud's birth mother—or, a woman who claims to be his birth mother—showing up recently out of the blue, and getting in touch with Bobby, for no particular reason that we know of.

"Third, we have Rachel Driver arriving from UCLA to teach at Cushing for the semester.

"Fourth, we have the victim's romantic involvement with Bobby McCloud.

"Finally, we have a story that comes out about Bobby in *People Magazine*, where he speaks publicly for the first time in his life about being adopted." She paused.

"What do you think?" she said.

"Keep going," Will replied.

"Now, let me put the stories in a different order," she said.

"Rachel and Gus have a baby twenty some years ago. Rachel didn't tell him she was pregnant, because they were splitting up, so Gus probably never even knew there was a child. Gus eventually transitions to Fanny Spendlove, and starts seeing Bobby McCloud. Bobby does an interview for *People Magazine*, and talks about his adoption. Rachel Driver reads the article, and shows up here in New Guilford. Bobby McCloud gets contacted by his birth mother for the first time in his life, and she asks to meet with him. Fanny Spendlove gets murdered.

"Let's imagine Rachel Driver's baby grows up to be Bobby McCloud," Edwina said. "Bobby gets involved with Fanny, who—unbeknownst to either of them—is actually Gus Prestopino, Bobby's own father. Rachel, Bobby's birthmother, reads the magazine interview, recognizes the name of the couple who adopted and raised her baby, and realizes Bobby is her son. And, when the magazine article goes on to mention Bobby's involvement with a certain host on GHN, Rachel goes nuts, lest the host in question should turn out to be Fanny Spendlove, whom Rachel has recognized as being Gus Prestopino, her ex-husband, and the father of her baby. What to do? She gets a job at Cushing for the semester because of its proximity to GHN. She confronts Fanny, learns of the affair with Bobby, and kills her."

"Why do you think Rachel wanted to get in touch with Bobby McCloud?" Will said. "To tell him that Fanny is really his own father?"

"Maybe," Edwina said. "Or maybe she just wanted to see her long-lost son, face to face, like a mother would. It's too ghoulish to think she was going to actually tell him he was sleeping with his biological father. I think Rachel probably wanted to see her baby boy in the flesh, all grown up, out of curiosity, or maybe out of a sense of loss and yearning for her long-lost motherhood. Like you told me, Rachel lost track of Bobby when he went into show business as a teenager, because he changed his name from Hanes to McCloud. She was probably so excited to find him that she was compelled to see him, *had* to see him. Maybe she wanted to make amends—to apologize for giving him up as a baby. Who knows?"

"The cone snail thing still bothers me as a method. It just doesn't make sense. I'll definitely bring Rachel in for questioning, though," Will said.

"Uh, about that, Will," Edwina said. "As a favor to the college—to me—is there some way you could do it quietly, and not have the entire police force descend on Sanborn House when you go to pick her up? The college doesn't need the publicity of one of their own being taken away in handcuffs. Think you could pick her up at her home?"

***

Rachel was dressed in sweatpants, flip-flops, and an oversized, button down men's shirt when the police showed up at her house. She was at first confused, and then belligerent. When asked if she'd be willing to accompany them to the police station to discuss the Fanny Spendlove investigation, she reluctantly agreed, under protest.

Val and Will faced Rachel across the table in the interrogation room.

"So, what's this all about?" Rachel said.

"It has come to our attention," Val said, "that you were acquainted with the victim in our current murder investigation, Fanny Spendlove, née Gus Prestopino. We believe you were married to Mr. Prestopino at one time. Is that correct?"

Despite the seriousness of the situation, Rachel affected an air of faint amusement. Her attitude seemed inexplicably dismissive.

"Yes, that's right," she chuckled. "Gus and I were married for almost five years. That was a long time ago, though. Another lifetime."

"Had you kept in touch?" Val asked.

"Hardly," Rachel said. "I hadn't thought about Gus in years. I had no idea—or interest, for that matter—where he was living, or what he was doing, or if he had remarried, or anything. He wasn't on my radar at all. I was more interested in getting on with my life. And I certainly didn't know anything about his plans for the sex-change thing."

"But you learned of it at some point?" Val said.

"Indeed, I did," Rachel said. "I recognized him on television—on GHN. He made a pretty decent looking woman, I must say. I mean, I knew Gus was rethinking his preference in sexual partners, but I was surprised to learn he'd actually undergone gender reassignment surgery."

"How did you feel about that?" said Val.

Rachel shrugged. "It's his life. No skin off my nose."

"You don't seem in the least upset by Fanny's death," Will said.

"I'm not," Rachel replied. "I'm sorry she's dead, but there was no love lost between us. As I say, another lifetime."

"How, exactly, did you find out about the gender reassignment surgery?" Val said.

"After I recognized Gus—as Fanny—on GHN, I contacted him, and asked to see him," Rachel replied.

"Why?" Will asked.

"Out of curiosity, I suppose," she said.

"Miss Driver," Val said, annoyed by Rachel's blithe affect, and wishing to blow it out of the water by ratcheting things up, "do you have any children?"

Rachel's bland expression withered.

"What's that got to do with anything?" she said.

"Possibly nothing," Val said.

Rachel gazed slowly around the drab, institutional room, and let out a deep sigh.

"Oh, what's the point of lying about it?" she said. "You already seem to know the answer. I got pregnant shortly before Gus and I split up. I never told him about it, because I had no plans to keep the baby, so what reason was there to tell him?

"When I happened to read an article in *People Magazine* about Bobby McCloud, I instantly recognized the name of his adoptive parents, and I knew Bobby must be the baby I gave away.

"Imagine that; my son, a movie star. The article went on to mention that Bobby was dating an older woman, a presenter on GHN. Thinking about the possibility that the older woman might be Fanny Spendlove made my skin crawl, and I had to find out.

"I met Fanny for coffee. It was so surreal," Rachel said. "She didn't want to meet me at GHN, which I completely understood. Too many uncomfortable questions to answer if we were seen together, I guess, so we met at some crappy diner out of town.

"When I told her about who Bobby actually was, Fanny got furious, and accused me of making the whole thing up, just to 'eff' with her for walking out on me. I told her that was preposterous—why would I want to do something like that after all these years—but she would not accept what I was telling her. I don't know if she thought I was lying about Bobby being our son, or if she couldn't process what I was saying, or just refused to let it sink in."

"I went on to say," Rachel said, "that if she continued to see Bobby I would report her to the authorities for incest. I think I probably threatened to do more than that, but I can't remember exactly everything I said. I was determined to put a stop to it"

"Did you make good on your threats?" Will asked.

"Of course not!" Rachel said. "I said my piece to Fanny, and I knew that's all I could do. I tried to make her promise never to see Bobby again—I said everything I could think of to persuade her. That was it.

Then I left. Besides, do I really look like a murderer to you?"

"That's the thing," Val said, "you do. You'd be surprised how many murderers look just like you. Nice and normal. It's the damnedest thing."

Rachel glared at Val.

"So," Val continued, "let me follow up on something Detective Tenney was getting at a moment ago. Once again: did you have anything to do with Fanny's death? And, by the way—just so you know—I would want to kill my ex-husband if he slept with one of our kids, too."

"Absolutely not," Rachel repeated. "I had nothing whatsoever to do with it. I wanted to, but I don't believe in going around killing people. I'm an academic, not a hit man."

"So," Val said, "we're meant to believe that you found out your ex-husband—now living as a woman—was sleeping with the son you had together, and you had nothing to do with her death?"

"Call it bad luck," Rachel said. "It's my bad luck to look so obviously like the murderer. But I'm telling you, I'm not. I wish I could tell you who was."

"Well, Professor Driver, be that as it may, we'll still need to keep you here a little while longer for further questioning," Val said.

CHAPTER 29

Slowly, slowly, catchee monkey.
~ Anon.

Once again, Edwina decided to wake Will from a deep sleep in the early morning. It had become a habit.

"You awake?" she jostled him gently. "Sorry, but I need to talk to you."

"What time is it?" he mumbled.

"It's not *that* early—it's almost time to get up," she said.

Will propped himself up, and squinted at the clock.

"No, it isn't," he said, and fell back onto the pillow.

"Yeah, but now you're awake, anyway," she said stubbornly. "And besides, it's about the case."

Will didn't move, so Edwina got out of bed, and went downstairs. The kitchen was chilly at that hour. She fed logs into the fire, filled the kettle, and set it atop the wood stove. She pulled a wool wrap around her, and rinsed the previous day's tea leaves out of the brown teapot.

Within minutes she could hear Will stirring upstairs. He appeared in the kitchen a few moments later, yawning. By the time the tea was poured, the kitchen was warm, and he was fully awake.

"I was thinking about how you said that Fanny was blackmailing Brad Pilfer," Edwina began, "and that there might be other people she was blackmailing besides him. Blackmail victims have very good motives for killing people, so I started to wonder who else there might be.

"I started by thinking about all the things you could blackmail somebody for—sex—drugs—a criminal background—plagiarism. Then I started thinking about Jimmy Lopez showing up in New Guilford out of the blue, that day you ran into him at Dan's. A seemingly random event.

"At first we figured his relationship with Don was going south because of the strain of the NSA stuff, remember? But, next thing you know, Jimmy calls you and says Don confessed to him, and that he—Don—had been involved with Fanny Spendlove back when she was Gus Prestopino, and Don was worried it would come out during the investigation, and damage his reputation and his career. Jimmy presented that as the reason for Don's skittish moods.

"But, what if Jimmy was wrong about the reason for the change in Don's behavior? What if Don lied to him about it, and what if Don's meltdown was actually not over the fact that he had had an affair with Gus Prestopino, but that he had murdered Fanny?"

"Think about this," she said. "If Gus Prestopino did have an affair with Don Gaylord all those years ago at that conference in San Francisco, then Fanny could easily have been blackmailing Don over it. Don would do just about anything to protect his career, even if it meant getting rid of Fanny. There's his motive."

"What about Rachel Driver as the murderer?" Will said.

"Hear me out," Edwina replied.

"Okay," she said, "so now we're able—theoretically, at least—to connect Don Gaylord to Fanny's murder. Now, for the NSA piece.

"You told me that Toby, your M.E., mentioned something about the government conducting experiments with cone snail toxins. Now, here's something we haven't considered: toxins are chemical compounds, and chemistry is Don Gaylord's bailiwick. If it's true that Don had hoped to become part of Phil Kimby's team at The Agency, I bet he would have submitted his new book as a calling card. His book clearly establishes him as an expert in biochemistry, organic and inorganic chemistry, physical chemistry—you name it. But Phil Kimby knows how unstable Don is, and that's why Don would never make the cut. Don't forget—I always thought Don was jealous and resentful of me when he heard Phil Kimby had tapped me for the NSA. Knowing Don, I can easily imagine that he wanted revenge—the way narcissists do when they're crossed or criticized, or rejected."

"I just reread his book. Guess what Chapter Nine includes?" Edwina said. "*Conus Geographus* studies—the Latin name for 'cone snail'.

"Here's another thing. I remember Phil Kimby asking me about Fanny's death when I saw him in Boston," she said. "I wondered why it would be of so much interest to Phil. Now I think it was because he might have suspected that Donald had something to do with Fanny's death. Phil would have known how furious Donald was about the NSA appointment not happening. Phil would have read Donald's new book. He put two and two together."

Neither spoke for a minute as Will processed the information.

"What do you think?" Edwina said.

"How do we put Gaylord at the GHN Studio, dropping a cone snail into the aquarium?" Will said.

Edwina shrugged.

"That's your department," she said. "I'm sure you'll figure it out."

CHAPTER 30

What worries you, masters you.
~ John Locke

Chief Burnstein and Will faced Donald Gaylord in the interrogation room. A pitcher of water and a stack of paper cups sat on the table between them.

"First of all, Professor Gaylord," Val said, "thank-you for agreeing to come in and speak with us. We understand what a busy schedule an international scholar like yourself has, and we're grateful for your time."

"Not at all," Donald replied, "not at all."

"We understand you're in the middle of a book tour?" she said.

"Yes, that's right. I'm due to speak at several more universities and institutions in Europe over the next few months. It's a very demanding schedule."

"Well," Val said, "we'll try not to take up any more of your time than we have to. Were you acquainted with Fanny Spendlove, sir?" she asked.

"Who?" Donald said. "Is that some sort of a joke?"

"It's not a joke, sir; no," Val said. "Miss Spendlove was a television personality on the home shopping television network. We're looking into her death. Are you aware of the case?"

"I'm afraid not," Donald replied. "Although I'm sure it has a certain small town appeal, I don't make a habit of reading the local paper."

"That's funny," Will said, "because we think you knew the victim. Could you be mistaken about that?"

"Mistaken?" Donald said.

"Yes, sir," Will said.

"What would make you think a man like myself would have any connection to—what did you call her—'a television personality'?" Donald said. "Unless her hobby was theoretical cosmology, I really can't imagine how my path would cross with someone who sells merchandise on television, can you?"

Will and Val regarded him evenly, allowing time for the weight of his words to saturate the atmosphere in a way that might start to discomfit to him.

"Well, sir," Will said, "for one thing, the victim was blackmailing you, wasn't she?"

Donald looked at Val and Will blankly.

"What did you say her name was?" he asked.

"Fanny Spendlove," Val replied. "Ring a bell?"

"The name is utterly preposterous!" Donald said.

"What makes you say that?" Will said.

Donald laughed.

"Do I really have to spell it out for you?" he asked. "It's rather crass."

"Humor us, Professor," Val said. "You're an educated man, much more so than Detective Tenney, here, or myself. Please, enlighten us."

"Very well. Apparently you aren't aware of the fact that in Britain, 'fanny' is a slang term for female genitalia, and 'Spendlove'....well, I'm sure you must see what I mean? The name is like an advertisement for some sort of sex worker. It's obviously a made-up name."

"That's very interesting," Val said, "but what makes you say the name was adopted? Maybe it was her real name."

"I just assumed," he said. "It has the ring of a stage name."

"No, sir, I don't think you did assume," Val said. "I think you knew for a fact that was not her given name."

"Did I?" Donald said.

"Yes," Val answered. "The reason being, that you knew her from before."

"From before?" Donald said.

"From before she worked at GHN—from before she was a woman," Val said. "You knew her back in the days when she was Gus Prestopino."

The interrogation room fell silent except for the low hum of the tape recorder. Val pushed side-by-side photos of Fanny Spendlove and Gus Prestopino across the table toward Donald Gaylord. She and Will sat back. They had all the time in the world.

"So," Donald said, "old Gus reinvented himself as a woman, did he? How about that?"

"But you already knew that," Val said, "long before now. Fanny was blackmailing you over the affair you and she had years ago when she was living as Gus Prestopino."

"That's why you got so spooked when Rachel Driver showed up at Cushing," Will said.

"What are you talking about?" Donald said. "Why would I get 'spooked'—as you call it—by a second rate academic like Rachel? No, I don't think so. I really have no idea what you're talking about."

"She's Gus's ex-wife," Will said. "But, you knew that. You would have recognized her from the conference at the Embarcadero Center years ago. And you must have wondered what she was doing here in New Guilford. It probably drove you crazy trying to figure out if her arrival had something to do with your affair with Gus."

"I'm afraid you're barking up the wrong tree," Donald said. "Why not question Rachel Driver? Isn't she the obvious suspect for her ex-husband's murder?"

"As a matter of fact, she's been cleared from the investigation," Will replied. "Turns out, she has a rock solid alibi."

"The truth is, Professor," Val said, "we have enough evidence to arrest you right now for Fanny's murder. So, why don't you do yourself and us the favor of walking us through what happened, instead of drawing this thing out any longer than necessary."

"This is patently ridiculous—nothing more than wild, conspiracy talk," Donald said. "I have nothing to do with any of this. Perhaps I should have a lawyer present."

"That's fine," Will said. "You have every right to do so, but we think it would help matters if you told us about your dealings with the NSA. You see, we did think Rachel Driver was involved in the death of Fanny Spendlove, until we realized there was something connecting the way Fanny was killed and current research going on at the NSA. You're the only individual that connects the two."

The atmosphere in the room shifted abruptly, as if a ticking bomb had quietly rolled under the table. Donald's rage was now palpable as he peered into the middle-distance, as if he were waiting for some sign of telepathic guidance. Neither Val nor Will spoke. They knew Donald was deciding his next move, and it was never a good idea to interrupt a suspect at such moments. You never knew what information was going to ride in on a big wave of emotion.

"To be clear," Donald said, "you should understand that the NSA is an outfit of incompetents run by a group of cretins. I had to prove definitively to those idiots how wrong they were to reject me from their ranks. I'm a molecular quantum mechanics expert, for god's sake! Who better to work on quantum cryptography for our national security?"

"Hard to figure, isn't it?" Val said. "A scientist of your stature and fame, with more qualifications than anybody."

"Precisely!" Donald said. "They were so, tragically wrong to reject me! I really don't know what they could have been thinking. I had no other recourse than to punish them for their ineptitude and poor judgment. Not to mention, for putting our country in harm's way by ignoring my contributions.

"Forgive me, but if I do say so myself, the jewel in the crown of my brand of genius in this situation was using the Agency's own research in my little demonstration. I decided to remove Fanny Spendlove from the picture by employing a method from the NSA's own playbook. They've been conducting research into the various applications of cone snail toxins for years, you know. All very hush-hush, of course."

"How did you go about securing the snail?" Will said.

"I purchased it on the internet, and had it shipped to a post office box under an alias," he replied, his eyes flashing. "The box was registered to 'Dr. Able Gunturmass'. Do you see? It's an anagram for Albertus Magnus, the brilliant theologian, philosopher, and chemist in the Middle Ages. He became beatified as a saint, you know!"

Val shot a glance at Will.

"How did you go about getting a cone snail into the aquarium before Fanny's show?" she asked.

Donald's face lit up.

"Child's play!" he replied. "Once Fanny got in touch, and tried to extort money from me, her days were numbered. The vault clanged shut, right then and there. She had sealed her own fate without even realizing it. I began watching and studying her on television, learning anything and everything I could. It was when she started promoting the aquarium show that I got the idea. By then I had read about the NSA doing research into possible applications for cone snail toxins. Chemistry is my specialty, you know, and I have been carefully following their research into chemical weaponry for years. After that, like any good operative, I simply did my due diligence, and learned all about these beautiful, deadly, little, sea demons."

Donald was clearly happy in the spotlight. He pushed his chair back from the table, and continued his narrative, pacing back and forth, as if delivering a seminal lecture in front of an audience. His sudden gestures and increasingly wild-eyed expressions gave the performance a manic quality.

"The next piece fell into place when GHN started making announcements about an upcoming studio tour. My opportunity was suddenly staring me in the face. It was terribly exciting. I scoured Fanny's GHN page every day. I noticed there was one particular name that kept popping up on her fan board. That's where Amaleen Stuckey came in. When I discovered she was on the tour list, I got in touch with her, and knowing of her demented devotion to Fanny, I presented myself as Fanny's cousin. I asked if she would be willing to help me play a little joke on my 'cousin', and she was delighted—stupid woman! The poor, lonely creature was so obviously infatuated with Fanny, I knew I would be able to easily manipulate her to do whatever I needed.

"I told Miss Stuckey that my 'cousin' had been afraid of snails ever since we were little kids, and wouldn't it be funny to slip one into the aquarium, and see what happened on live air? I shipped the snail to Miss Stuckey with precise instructions about how to handle it, and she carried out my every directive to a tee. I told her how to safely transport the snail, what to do when she got to the studio—and most importantly of all—not to tell anyone about our private joke. Absolutely no one.

"She turned out to be a very adept conspirator, and managed easily to separate herself from the tour group for just long enough to drop the snail into the tank."

"But then, afterwards, you had to get rid of her, so there would be no link back to you?" Val added.

"Collateral damage. Couldn't be helped," Donald said, fluffing his pocket handkerchief. "It was laughably easy. All I had to do was access her GHN shopping history. I purchased a box of the type of candies she had ordered repeatedly, spiced them up with a little chemical concoction of my own invention, and—'goodnight, Miss Stuckey'—see you in my dreams!"

"How did you know Fanny would pick the snail up?" Will asked.

"Oh, that," Donald said. "Yes, I had to think about that for a while. In the end, all it took was a phone call to the little man in the control room who gives directions to the presenters via earpiece. He tells them when to take calls, what to emphasize in order to boost sales, and so forth. I introduced myself as the aquarium's designer. I told him our research definitively shows that sales are directly correlated to what's on display inside the tanks when potential customers view them. I made him promise me that when the tank was presented on GHN, the large snail with colorful markings would be held up for the audience to admire. I guaranteed him it would send sales through the roof.

"All you have to do is watch GHN, and observe carefully," he said. "The tricks of the trade are all right there in front of you—there's no great mystery to it. It's not rocket science, you know!"

"So, by getting Fanny out of the way, you accomplished two goals with one strike, is that right?" Will said. "Your career and reputation were safe from Fanny's threats, and by the same token, you were able to show the NSA how clever and superior you are."

"Exactly! It was wonderfully efficient. I knew that when those dullards from The Agency got wind of what I'd accomplished, they would come crawling back," Donald said. "After all, now I can take sole credit for administering the first intentional casualty ever from cone snail poison."

The interview went on for some time, fuelled by a highly energized Donald, eager to dazzle his audience with each and every detail of his daring, one-man espionage operation. The subject of bringing in a lawyer never came up again.

CHAPTER 31

*The nitrogen in our DNA, the calcium in our teeth, the
iron in our blood, the carbon in our apple pies were
made in the interiors of collapsing stars. We are made
of starstuff.*
~ Carl Sagan

His department colleagues—along with the rest of
the Cushing community—reeled in collective disbelief
from the news of the allegations brought against Donald
Gaylord. As far as speaking to the press went, or to
anyone outside the department, they closed ranks.
Department Head Helen Mann had to be hospitalized
briefly for a nervous disorder relapse, but she was soon
back on the job, meeting with a top PR firm in Boston
about how best to minimize the impact of the scandal
on the college's reputation and financial donations from
alumni. Her first allegiance was to Cushing, and
protecting her beloved institution from this current
disgrace became something of a renewed calling for
Professor Mann. Once she had recovered fully from her
mental health setback, she experienced a kind of rebirth
along with a heightened sense of purpose. She would
protect Cushing College to the death.

Hoping to meet the need for some kind of emotional
outlet, and to provide a modicum of closure to this sad
business, Paolo and Francesca Rossetti invited the
whole department to their home for dinner shortly after
Donald's arrest, where everyone could be together in a
homey, relaxed atmosphere, and talk about it—or not

talk about it—as they liked, and be of support to one another.

The evening proved to be all of that. The entire department showed up, and none empty-handed. Nedda Cake brought two loaves of her Welsh spotty bread; Will made pot roast; Edwina baked cookies; Helen Mann arrived with a case of wine; and so on. Many stayed until the wee hours. Edwina and Will reached out to Jimmy Lopez, but he declined the invitation. There was much eating and drinking, accompanied by dancing, and even a few tears.

Rachel Driver returned to California before the semester ended, cutting her allotted time at Cushing short. Because Rachel had appeared prominently as a witness during the trial, she and Helen Mann agreed that her continued presence at Cushing would prolong negative publicity for the college, and delay the scandal being put to rest. Rachel's residency at Sanborn House meant there were always reporters lurking around, attempting to waylay Rachel for an interview, or hoping to dig up more dirt about the case. With Rachel soon gone, and with Lois Leiberman and Seth Dubin still away on sabbatical, Helen asked others on the staff to cover the extra teaching duties. No one balked. Even Helen took on the responsibility of teaching an undergraduate course, something she had not done in many years. The journalists gradually stopped buzzing around Sanborn House, goings-on in the Department generally quieted down, and eventually things returned to normal.

For the most part, the lives of those involved in the investigation returned to normal, too. Out from under a cloud of suspicion—or perhaps, bolstered by it—Bobby McCloud's new movie raked in more than projected in its opening weekend, and the studio signed him on for three more projects. After the movie's debut, Bobby took an extended vacation in Australia with his scuba-diving dog, and his new girlfriend, but not before Harry Crassman had a chance to have her thoroughly investigated by a private detective.

Mary Lou Flowers continued on at GHN, drinking more than ever, and waging a daily battle against her burgeoning weight. Once she gave into the impulse to come on the air with a glass or two of wine already under her belt, viewers began calling and writing into the network, praising her noticeably renewed energy and good humor. With steady increases in her sales, GHN was forced to give her a raise, and offer her time slots of her own choosing. Mary Lou, a reluctant morning person, happily locked in afternoon show times exclusively, so she could freely enjoy her evenings drinking and watching television—lobbing insults at other presenters to her heart's content. Life was good.

And, once Brad Pilfer's wife had entirely forgiven him for his affair with Mary Lou, their marriage seemed to grow stronger than ever. Overcome with guilt, Brad broke things off with Mary Lou once and for all, and for good. Some months later, however, when a new vendor arrived to GHN in the form of Muffin Dorfman—sole creator and owner of a line of slimming undergarments, called Amen & Brallelujah!—VP Brad Pilfer soon found his way into a new dalliance.

***

Will and his neighbor, Cyrus Thetford, had worked every weekend one summer to carve out a hiking trail on the mountain where they lived not far from one another. Starting in the woods at the end of their road, they chopped down a swath of trees to the top of the mountain, charting an incline gentle enough so that even children could make their way to the summit. Armed with chainsaws, a two-cycle brush-cutter, loppers, and a pole-mounted pruning saw, Will and Cyrus had consumed countless sandwiches and bottles of Gatorade over the course of the trail's construction that hot summer. At the top of the mountain, the men had cleared a small glade, and installed a bench from which to view the 360 degree vistas of rolling hills, woods, and streams, and distant fields and valleys. Autumn was an especially popular time for the trail. The reward at the top for those who made the hike was an astonishing panorama awash in color.

Edwina and Will marked the end of the case by taking a few days off from work, and spending them at Will's house—going for walks; reading by the fire; cooking; sleeping late; and doing little bits of business around the house that needed attention.

The last night of their hiatus was bright and clear, and after dinner they hiked to the top of the mountain by the light of the brightly waxing moon. They had walked the trail many times before, but that night they dawdled along the way, taking time to savor the chill in the air, and the snaps and crunches of twigs underfoot, and the smell of the trees. When they reached the top, the sky opened up into an infinite, black dome lit by planets and stars.

"It's so hard to comprehend that Donald actually put a stop to the lives of two human beings," Edwina said, nestled against Will on the bench. "Someone I've worked with and known for years, capable of that. How will he cope with prison? I don't even like to think about it," she said.

"Maybe his lawyers will figure out a way to get him off," Will said. "Crazier things happen. You just never know. Val says his lawyers are considering an insanity defense, but I don't think they'll be able to make it fly."

"Why not?" Edwina said.

"It's not used all that much anymore, for the simple reason that it rarely works. It's hard to prove legal insanity in court," Will said. "But if they do go ahead with an insanity defense, Donald's paranoia should come in handy. New Hampshire is the only state left that uses the Durham rule to determine legal insanity, and it relies heavily on paranoia as a measure of whether or not you can be considered nuts."

"Do you think Donald is insane?" she said.

"Nah. I think he's a narcissist—he's neurotic, not crazy. Donald, and nobody else but Donald, is responsible for his actions. It was all his own choice, every step of the way."

The pine trees shuddered in the breeze. Distant, yellow lights from a smattering of houses peeked through the trees across the valley. As far as they could see, the whole world seemed to be tucked up for the night. Will wrapped his arms around Edwina.

"So, what're we looking at?" he said, gazing upward.

"Oh, lots of amazing stuff," Edwina said.

"For instance, did you know that stars don't really twinkle? They just look like they do. If you and I were sitting on a bench in outer space right now, instead of on top of this mountain, they wouldn't be twinkling at all."

"Why?" Will said.

"Because, there's no atmosphere out there," Edwina replied. "If we were out in space right now, the starlight would appear to us steady and fixed. But, because the earth has lots of atmosphere around it, light from stars has to pass through all sorts of atmospheric turbulence, which acts like a prism, and it jiggles and shifts the starlight around. Hence, twinkling."

"What else?" Will said.

"Let's see...." Edwina said. "You know about space and time being intertwined, right?"

"Yeah," Will replied. "No, actually, but go on."

"So, as you and I," she said, "sit here looking out at the universe, we're actually looking back in time. Reason being, it takes such a long time for the image of something out in space to reach our eyeballs, we can say we're seeing images from the past. That's how great the distances are. The sun, for instance, is only about 93,000,000 miles away, but if it exploded, we wouldn't even know about it for eight minutes. That's how long it takes for light to travel from the sun to the earth.

"Isn't it wonderful?" she said breathlessly.

Besotted, Will watched as water vapor condensed into fog when she exhaled.

"If we had a powerful enough telescope, and we took it with us 65,000,000 light years away from the earth, we could actually look back at the earth, and see the dinosaurs," she said.

"Incredible," Will said.

"Or, take the Andromeda galaxy, which is a particularly beautiful spiral galaxy, like the Milky Way," she said. "When we look at it through the telescope, we're seeing it as it was two million years ago, because that's how long its image takes to reach the earth. So there you have it: space and time, intertwined.

"We know a fair bit about the universe," she said, "and we're discovering the most amazing, new stuff every, single day."

The temperature was dropping, and it was time to head home.

Part way down the trail, Edwina experienced a sudden, momentary sensation of sublime metamorphosis—as if she and Will, and the stars and trees and mountain were all one and the same, all connected. It filled her with unaccountable joy, and then the feeling was gone. Coyote calls penetrated the night.

It was the final night of their rural idyll. In the morning they would drive back to New Guilford—back to civilization—and return to work. Will's house was warm and welcoming. The glowing embers in the fireplace, no longer with sufficient combustion to produce flames, still radiated as much heat as a roaring fire. Will locked up the house for the night, and they got ready for bed. The windows in the sleeping loft looked out onto acres of woods filled with sugar maples, white ash, and beech trees, now all under the cover of darkness. The sweet smell of apple wood filled the air.

"I wish we had a few more days to ourselves," Will said. "Can't say I'm looking forward to going into the office tomorrow."

"Oh, Will," she replied, snuggling under the quilt. "Don't you know there's no such thing as tomorrow? It's only a concept—an illusion—a dream, really. It doesn't even exist. Now, what possible purpose would it serve to trouble ourselves over something that isn't real?"

By way of elaboration, Edwina endeavored to engage Will's focus so completely, that, indeed, tomorrow ceased to exist for them. There was only now.

THE END

ABOUT THE AUTHOR

 Elissa D. Grodin is a children's author and novelist, and has written for the *Times Literary Supplement*. She lives in New York City and Connecticut with her husband, actor/commentator/activist Charles Grodin. Her first cozy mystery *Physics Can Be Fatal*, introduced her heroine Edwina Goodman.

www.ingramcontent.com/pod-product-compliance
Lightning Source LLC
Chambersburg PA
CBHW020321260626
47156CB00004B/1324